Wellness Magick

Sophie L. Robinson-Matthews

This text is not intended to replace the guidance of your medical professional

ISBN: 978-1-913479-25-1 (paperback)

ISBN: 978-1-913479-26-8 (ebook)

That Guy's House

20-22 Wenlock Road

London

England

N1 7GU

www.thatGuysHouse.com

That Guy's House

DEDICATION

Here's to all those who have always known there was something better for them. To all the people who have ever felt 'odd' and only want to be themselves. To all of those who are walking their own path. May everyone who reads this live with authenticity, balance, love, a sprinkle of magick, and have the confidence to express your True Magickal Self.

I choose to consciously and actively influence my life experience, by filling my mind with uplifting thoughts and images, feeling gratitude and following joy, and moving forwards in ways that support my personal path of fulfilment.

CONTENTS

Authenticity is when you say and do the things you actually believe.
– Simon Sinek

ACKNOWLEDGMENTS

With many thanks to the amazing Emma Mumford for all of her advice and support to me whilst writing this book – you are an inspiration for honesty and the book-midwife that made birthing this book a reality! Thank you to Jesse Lynn Smart who was the first proof-reader of this book and whose help and care is greatly appreciated. With great gratitude to my loved ones for your support and role in my evolution, and to friends, both online and offline, who have encouraged me always. A very special thank you and love to my wonderful husband who has held me emotionally and physically through everything and without whom this book would not have been the enjoyable process that it was – you are eternally my favourite human. Thank you to my clients, who humble me with their trust and inspire me to keep walking this path. A special thank you to those of you on my journey who have believed in and encouraged me; there are so many of you, I can't name you all, but I trust that you know who you are and I am grateful for you. With particular thanks to Kelly-Ann Maddox who granted me permission to use her card spreads in this book and who is an all-round tenaciously inspiring witchy-woman! I can't thank the amazing Fiona Horne enough for her books and music which have been pillars to me for so long and feel like a part of my soul. And thank you to all the other writers who have inspired me through their books, to the researchers who do the hard work of discovering what helps, and to the Universe for always having my back…

1 ~ INTRODUCTION

Those who don't believe in magic will never find it.
– Roald Dahl

Hello, dear reader, and thank you for choosing this book! My intention is for you to gain a solid foundation in your own *personal* mental wellness. The melding of spiritual and research-based psychological tools and knowledge within a Wiccan-spiritual framework has served me well, and I hope that it will serve you too, as you have been drawn to this book for a reason.

With the greatest love I say that if you are truly feeling terrible and that you may cause harm to yourself, please, please reach out to someone. There will be someone who can help you, whether they are at a medical centre near you or at an organisation on the other end of a helpline. If you're reading this and feel so very low, then let this be the sign of permission to reach out and get that help now. No one has to walk a path of healing in isolation; it's much easier with the right support, however that looks for you. With that said, I hope this book leaves you feeling empowered and hopeful that you can change what is happening in your mind and your life to live in authenticity and congruence to you.

I refer to the Universe, Cosmos, Spirit, divinity, God, and Goddess collectively to mean that force of unfathomable cosmic synchronicity and mystery that gives our world its beautiful magick. Replace accordingly with whatever feels best for you. If you're not comfortable with those terms, or if they have no meaning or place for you, that's ok – they didn't for a time for me either. I simply used to think of my Higher Self instead. Everyone's journey is unique, and that includes what words feel right for us. Also, for clarity, spirituality to me is the embodiment of deepening self-awareness, our connection to our Higher and True Self, divinity and the natural world around us. It is also empowering you to form your own beliefs that evolve as you evolve. It helps you to cope in the world and with the inevitabilities of life, such as death. Spirituality is our relationship with our Self, our way of navigating life and the world around us; it's the practices as well as the beliefs and personal morals we hold. It is the journey of getting to know yourself and through that, actualising your greatest potential. It's not just about meditating, rituals and daily practices – it's about facing your truth.

On the following pages you will firstly find a brief memoir of my journey so far, which I hope will inspire you and help you realise that no matter the shape of the path of your life so far, you do have the power to change how you think and feel about yourself and your life and to influence how others respond to you. I show you that in having self-belief, self-trust, and most importantly, self-love, together with faith in the Universe, you can do anything you set your mind to, and that it is a great thing to accept help from others rather than prolong a struggle by being on your own.

The second part is the wellness magick. I take you through the practices, tools, methods, and knowledge that helped me create mental wellness and balance in my life. With each practice, I encourage you to give it a *fair chance* to take effect. It is incredibly rare in life that anything is done once and then the problem is solved forever. We do not shower once and remain clean for the rest of our life. A lot of these things are called *practices* because they are things to do regularly in order to get the maximum benefit from them. It is a myth that a habit is formed in 21 days. In reality, research has now shown that it depends on the habit and the individual; but if something has the power to change your life for the better, then I believe it is worth giving a fair chance, whether that's a few attempts or trying it for a few weeks – give things a go and see how they work for you. I know that I'm not alone in struggling with, for example, passive meditation in the beginning; but persistence with it and *knowing* it was so beneficial for my wellness meant that I got to see and feel the benefits of it eventually, and it didn't take as long as I thought!

It can also be the case that, for example, you're trying a technique to help you with low mood, and you try it when you're at a 5 (if you scale that feeling from 0-10) and it doesn't feel like it's helped. However, if you try it again when you're at a 3, you might feel a difference. This is all about self-awareness, and because it is very difficult to distinguish all these nuances and remember them, if you are going to take your wellness journey and yourself seriously, then writing them down will be important to you. In doing so, you can give yourself feedback for how you're doing, how things are working for you and why, and have that time for reflection to review progress. You'll have a physical record of what's going on in your mind, body, life, and the actions you have taken, and not have to rely on memory accuracy and recall abilities.

We carry inside us the wonders we seek outside us. – Rumi

For maximum effectiveness, you will want to dedicate a journal that you use alongside this book and use it to work through each chapter accordingly. If you want to read it through fully first and then work through it actively, that is great too! I will say though that those initial thoughts and feelings you experience whilst reading something for the first time can be invaluable. The goal of this book is to give you short-term strategies that have immediate or quick positive effects, giving you the mind space to orient yourself into a better position so that you can cultivate a practice that works for your *long-term* wellness.

I also advocate that you use your experience with each practice to start to create a personal toolbox of techniques that work well for you in different situations, so you know that whatever happens, you can handle any challenges and changes that occur with grace, love and respect.

At the end of each section, there are action points, which are specifically to encourage you to create something that can be added to your toolbox, and journal prompts. The prompts are to inspire you to expand your internal dialogue and go a little deeper into building your self-awareness and understanding, or to explore a perspective you may have around a particular topic. The purpose of the list of prompts is to give you an easy tool that you can use when necessary. However, my wish is that you do use them and do not just write them out and forget about them. Make them visible in your life, remind yourself they exist to help you, even take photographs of your lists on your mobile so that you have them with you. You can even collage or illustrate them, display them as art – make them appealing to use and memorable because they are so simple, yet so helpful.

The chapters follow the five elements present in Wicca, which gives the book its framework. You do not have to follow a Wiccan path or be a practitioner of witchcraft to benefit from this book; likewise, you can be an experienced practitioner. This book isn't a 'how-to' of magick or spirituality; however, you don't have to know much to benefit from the book – simply having an open mind and curiosity works wonders. For those who aren't sure on the terminologies: to explain, Wiccans practise witchcraft within the religion of Wicca, but you do not have to be Wiccan or religious to practice witchcraft. 'The Craft', as it's sometimes called, is outside of religion, and technically anyone of any faith or no faith can practice witchcraft. Being a witch is to create change within the natural cycles of the wild around and within. It is a process of developing belief and trust – within and without – finding out who you are at your most authentic expression.

Those familiar with tarot will notice the similarities between the elements and the suits of the cards. Earth is pentacles/coins, Water is chalices/cups, Air is swords/arrows, and Fire is wands/sticks. If you understand the suits, you already have some natural understanding of the elements and can use your cards to add a further dimension while following this book to create a wellness foundation.

Participate relentlessly in the manifestation of your own blessings.
– Elizabeth Gilbert

If you are firmly on a magickal path and have ideas of your own correspondences, then please use what works for you instead of the suggested correspondences I make. For those of you who have no idea what I mean by correspondences, these are attributes assigned to a particular object or phenomenon, such as colour, the day of the week, numbers, the Moon phase, time of day, direction, herbs, scents, etc., and they are used in magickal practices to assist with setting intention and assigning further meaning to what you are doing. If you have not developed your own personal correspondences, I suggest them where appropriate in the book based upon either my own experience or what is commonly attributed within the witchy/spiritual community. However, always remember that magick is not from the tools and ingredients – it is from *you.* The items in spellcraft and ritual act as signals and symbols of your intent to further clarify to the Universe and/or your deeper Self that you want change and to see it manifest or be made physical. This is the connection between will and action, the corporeal and the material – this is magick. Magick is usually hidden in the in-betweens … It is the art of changing consciousness at will.

It is extremely important to note that with anything that you may ingest, inhale, or apply to the skin, check that you or members of your household (including animals) do not have any contraindications or allergies to said ingredient and that it is safe to use for your present condition. Certain herbs are said to not be safe if you are pregnant or on particular types of medications. Do your research, consult a medical doctor if in doubt, and always make sure safety is observed foremost.

Within each elemental section, there will be sub-sections that take you through tasks and practices to do for each of these further four areas: internal, external, mental, and physical. This relates to a principal in occultism and Wicca, 'As within, so without; as above, so below.' This phrase relates to an understanding that our actions affect our outside world, and that often we are mirrors of our external world and vice versa. It is the invisible link between us and everything. It shows us that we can change things and ourselves and we are not simply at the mercy of things as they are. It is a hopeful concept for many and is the basis of magick and philosophies of the workings of the Universe.

Before we begin, let's just clarify wellness. I mean wellness to be a state of being that is free from mental anguish, self-bullying, turmoil, stress, and confusion. Instead, the mind is a place for ideas, able to problem-solve effectively, think rationally, peacefully, and calmly. This psychological wellness transpires into life wellness where you are able to act in a way that is for your highest good; you're clear on who you are, what you like and do not, what your boundaries and values are, and what your passions and direction are. You're able to give and receive love, implement effective coping strategies to handle challenges and hurts, and trust yourself and others appropriately. You feel that your energy and attention are going in the directions you want them to in your life, and you are able to live authentically to your true self.

As with any self-help book, it puts you, the reader, in the seat of power. *You* have the power over your own mind and autonomy within your life. You hold the key to change, and the key is through action. If you act on the things within this book, changes will take place. There are also complementary resources to this book for you that can be found online via my website, sophiewildrobin.com.

The other key is consistency. It is very rare in life that we do something once and that's it. We don't bathe once and become clean forever, or get on a bike for one minute and know how to ride it. Many of the techniques will be about you figuring out how you can start implementing them in your life. There is no rush, and you don't need to do everything all at once; in fact, it's much better if you take your time. It takes time to make lasting changes, and those changes are more likely to last if implemented gradually and sustainably. I wish you the best of success on your journey.

Authenticity, Balance, Love – Sophie *xo*

When you are born in a world you don't fit in, it's because you were born to help create a new one. – Johnny Stones

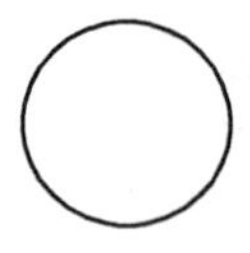

2 ~ MY JOURNEY, IN A NUTSHELL

You've seen my descent. Now watch my rising. - Rumi

I am Sophie, and by telling you how I arrived at this point now (of writing this book!), I hope to give the pages that follow some context. Everyone walks their own path, and my encouragement is to always do what is right for you as an individual. Pick what works for you from this book and leave what doesn't, perhaps for another time.

So, how did I 'get into all this spiritual and witchcraft stuff'? I can remember it like it was yesterday. It was the school spring break, and I had not long had my eleventh birthday. Eleven is well known to be a spiritual number, and it's also my life path number, for those who understand numerology. It relates to messages that call to the spirit, understanding of spiritual mysteries and sharing wisdom with others – all of which have been increasingly important aspects of my life and part of the reason for this book, I'm sure!

I was sitting in the garden as it was sunny, taking a break from revision by reading the last book of the *Chronicles of Narnia* by C. S. Lewis. After finishing the book, I zoned out, and I remember feeling as if everything was clicking into place, even if I didn't understand what the 'everything' was exactly. I have no idea why it was that book for my spiritual awakening to happen, but that's how it happened.

I soon went to my local library and took out a book on Egyptian gods and goddesses, then the Greek, then books on Feng Shui, Buddhism and many other various books in the 'Mind, Body, Spirit' section. Finally, I wandered to the 'Religion' section and was drawn to Phyliss Curott's book, *Book of Shadows - A Modern Woman's Journey into the Wisdom of*

Witchcraft and the Magic of the Goddess. This book was the permission I needed to accept that I held neo-Pagan beliefs and identified as a witch, and it gave me the courage to start truly walking my own path. Paganism resonated with me because I appreciated that it innately valued the physical, the corporeal, and the senses. I felt a great dissonance between what I felt was true and what I heard and saw with regards to the respect shown to the Earth, nature, and her creatures, and the respect shown to the body, especially the female body. Neo-Paganism was the first movement I'd come across that didn't seem to want to make me ashamed of parts of who I am and how I wanted to live my life.

Shortly after reading Phyliss's book, I took a trip into the local city with my parents and while they were drinking coffee in a bookstore, I was taking in the large selection of 'Mind, Body, Spirit' and 'Religion, Spirituality' books. I felt drawn to a bold book by Fiona Horne, simply entitled *Witch: A Magickal Journey.* I purchased it with my birthday money and was captivated. Fiona's band, *Def FX*, got me deeply in love with music and she became my idol – a real source of unlimited inspiration, and I credit her with being a huge factor in me finding my authenticity and being able to live it.

My parents resisted at first when I informed them I was Wiccan (as that label fitted me best back then) – fear was blocking them, but thankfully they didn't take much persuasion to open their minds a little, and they have supported me with my spirituality ever since. I read as widely as I could into other Pagan paths, both historic and modern, other esoteric and occult things, including divination. My mom took me sometime around my twelfth birthday to the local spiritual shop where I purchased my first tarot deck, dowsing pendulum, and a book by Sigmund Freud on dreams, which sparked my interest in psychology.

I can't go back to yesterday because I was a different person then.
– Alice Liddell

This is where it gets difficult to write because the following is the history that really only select people have heard before. (Sorry, Mom and Dad, if you read this, but no one's life is ever perfect, and regardless of anything, I love you both dearly.) I need to take you back to when I was *very young* to explain about my mental health. Someone I loved incredibly dearly and with whom I had a fierce bond passed away, but it wasn't handled in the best way by the adults around me (they did what they thought was best at the time). Consequently, this death impacted my world view more than it should have. I developed and performed secret 'rituals', and these turned into many different types of obsessions and compulsions so that no one else I loved would die (of course that's impossible, but as a child, it seemed as plausible as anything, plus I didn't understand obsessive-compulsive disorder then).

Now, I really enjoyed learning, and so I enjoyed that aspect of school until my best friend moved away, and I just had a hard time after that. I was continuously picked on by other kids; I never understood why. I guess I was just an easy target because I was a bit different and wasn't great at standing up for myself or ignoring people – they got to me a lot of the time, and I unwittingly fed them by giving them my reactions. This lowered my confidence. I had a much more pleasant time with adults and books. My parents eventually found out about the bullying in first school and made me take karate lessons, which helped with my self-confidence.

After first school, I had lots of close friends, but I always felt like I didn't quite fit in anywhere, floating between friend groups but never really having that solid bunch who have each other's backs through thick and thin. I grew apart from many friends over the years, and I learnt that it's better to have a few dependable and trustworthy friends that you can count on one hand over many when the quality isn't there. Not having people I could really trust, and being an only child, within me grew a deep loneliness and an increasing ego-need to prove that I didn't need anyone. This contradicted the fact that I was a hopeless romantic and bought into the idea of a soulmate who would understand you completely, and almost be a sort of salvation who would somehow erase all problems in your life.

The need for external validation came to a peak when I was fifteen. I worried about *everything* – I didn't know how to not worry or ruminate. It had become as natural and easy as breathing. The only time I felt really safe was in my bedroom, sitting in a circle, or in the garden, reading a book. I had a toxic friendship that led me to have a lot of fun but also do a lot of things I wouldn't have done if not for pressure and guilt-tripping, which didn't help with anxiety.

I soon entered an unhealthy relationship that involved gaslighting, which increased in intensity and insidiousness over time, wearing down my self-esteem and sense of self-worth. By this point, I firmly had generalised anxiety – I could have a full-blown panic attack at any moment – and the abusive relationship had caused me to develop body dysmorphia, and I gradually became depressed as I lost more and more of who I was. I went from someone who never cried to someone who cried at everything, and I could not take any kind of criticism, no matter how gently and constructively it was presented. It felt like my sparkle was wearing off, like a stone, but instead of being polished over time by the current in the stream, I was getting dinked and chinked and becoming spikey. The more I disliked myself, the worse I felt, and the worse I felt, the more I blamed myself for feeling that way, and so the cycle perpetuated. I realise now this person was reacting to a sense of abandonment, which was their issue, but it was affecting me, and I didn't know how to support that person back then; I just felt scared, trapped and powerless.

I felt more and more that my parents didn't really understand me either. After all, I was not being myself around anyone, and this meant I was not being kind to myself or anyone else really. I was very defensive and consistently on edge; I couldn't relax. Cracks started to grow into fissures. School got intense with exams, as it does, and the only person I felt like I could be a modicum of myself around became ill and passed away, a couple of days before my sixteenth birthday. Many traumatic memories were created during this time, and I was so full of shame that I didn't dare tell anyone around me how I was actually feeling, and I also didn't want to add to anyone else's problems. I had grown up hearing quips that negatively stereotyped emotional struggles and that people around me didn't '*believe* in depression, that it was for the weak'. I became pretty good at compartmentalising things so that I didn't draw attention to myself, and was able to put on the 'happy' face for others most of the time.

I had lost myself. All my magickal and wellness practices, like yoga, ground to a halt. I had forgotten who I was in my effort to try to be everything for everyone else. This is why authenticity, intuition, congruence, and love are such important concepts for me now. I know how life quickly loses its sparkle without these in place. I went on a downwards spiral, with my mental health getting worse each month; not sleeping, developing an unhealthy relationship with food simply because I needed to control *something*, and pushing friends away.

Happiness can be found even in the darkest of times if one only remembers to turn on the light. – Albus Dumbledore

I had always been a vivid dreamer and remembered my dreams most nights; however, I had a *lot* of reoccurring nightmares, so trying to understand that was really intriguing, as nothing I had done to help them had made much of a difference. I wasn't frightened of things you'd find in horror films. I'd also had encounters with spirits and loved to hear other people's paranormal stories; even if a lot were explainable, I still found it fun. My nightmares were the kind where you lose your voice when you need to shout for help, being stalked, attacked by faceless men, sometimes with knives, losing the ability to run away, or when I *could* run, falling down an endless black hole. Looking back, it's obvious what my subconscious was dealing with, but I was trying to ignore everything, to repress it. I had stopped caring so much about myself, saying yes to things I didn't want in a last-ditch effort to 'fit in', feeling isolated, invisible, and hating who I was. I felt like a duck on water – mostly calm on the surface, but going crazy underneath. I was punishing myself for existing, both mentally and physically.

Thankfully, my spark of curiosity about the world was not extinguished, and I still engaged well with my education, though I had definitely stopped trying so hard with most of the subjects. I was elated to pass maths so that I could take psychology classes in sixth form, as it was literally the only thing I actually had any interest in at that point. The reason for that was because through trying to understand my nightmares and get better at lucid dreaming when I wanted to, I discovered Sigmund Freud, who is a significant historical figure in psychology. I then started to think that psychology presented me with the hope that I could try to understand myself. My wonderful psychology teacher noticed something 'off' about me early on. She pushed me outside my comfort zone, making me answer questions in class, even though I didn't put my hand up, and reading examples of my work. She knew I was capable and, in her own way, she was helping me to build up my confidence and trust in myself again, helping me to find my voice.

One day, my psychology teacher told me she'd noticed the decline in my demeanour, and assured me that I didn't have to tell her what was going on if I didn't want to, but she offered to lend me a book from her personal bookcase. She never forced me to talk about anything or judged me; she only gave me hope and believed in me. One book jumped out at me: *Feel the Fear and Do It Anyway*, by Susan Jeffers. I got stuck into the book, and this experience was enough to be a turning point. Someone who didn't need to care about me had *seen* me.

Finally, I started to push back, and *the* breakup happened, and my word, was it messy and painful. Months of what can only be politely described as 'mind turmoil' ensued. It eventually exploded so far that there was no going back. I was done. I wrote a list of all the reasons I didn't want to, couldn't, and shouldn't be with him, and referred to it often to help me keep my motivation up. I did spells on myself and cord-cuttings to help me heal, anything I could think of to stop me turning back. I turned what I had felt into hate, steeled my heart and shut it off from love …

Eventually, my mom came up with a cup of tea and a bar of chocolate with a message she'd written on it. In her own way, she told me I couldn't keep going on like this, and she wanted me to get help. At the time, the words she said to me hurt, but in reality, it was what I needed to hear to realise I was at rock bottom. She was right – it was sink-or-swim time. After months of mostly feeling apathetic and zombie-like, I cried. I released all the crap and slept well for the first time in months.

We must all face the choice between what is right and what is easy.
– Albus Dumbledore

The next day, I woke up to the Sun shining brightly into my room (because I hadn't shut the curtains as the Moon was shining in the night before). I then heard my inner voice or Higher Self. For the first time in what felt like forever, that voice was louder than the vicious bully voice. (Note: this was still *my* voice, the one you think in words with inside your head; it wasn't a separate feeling as it can be with a hallucination or psychosis.) This higher voice parented me into getting myself up and starting my healing journey – properly this time.

I booked myself in to the doctor's because I was fed up of feeling anxious and depressed; however, he didn't 'believe in' mental health and only offered me medication, which I rejected because I knew it wasn't for me. I was determined in this instance to try without anything like that first. So, I remembered what I had enjoyed before. Who was I before I started to feel all this crap and believe all the horrid things? I got back into a regular witchcraft and spirituality practice, with divination, yoga, meditation, *reading*. I started to use all of the psychology I was learning to get myself to a point where I felt free of depression, body dysmorphia, and OCD, to heal trauma and my relationship with food.

I eventually dated again after the first relationship ended, trying really hard to not look at guys with a tainted lens. And while I was able to do that work and be able to see people as their own individuals and not cast a shadow on them from poor experiences with others, I didn't truly feel a spark from any of them. I worried that maybe I was destined to be a crazy cat lady after all, but somehow, I didn't quite believe that was true. When I was eighteen, I had gotten to a point where I was much happier with myself and within myself and had courage and confidence again to a better degree than I ever had.

One Friday night under a waxing Moon, I decided to write a list of qualities I thought I wanted in my dream guy. I burnt it, let it go and just forgot about it. A Moon cycle later, I was out with a friend, and out of nowhere, she told me to turn around quick and point at someone in the room. Without thinking, I did what she said, and my finger pointed squarely towards a tall guy with his back towards me. Next thing I knew she was pulling me towards him, had tapped him on the shoulder, pointed at me and declared, 'Meet your new girlfriend!' Needless to say that I was pretty embarrassed, but he was a good sport about it and we ended up talking all evening, swapping numbers and dating within a couple of days.

Suffice it to say that he had all the qualities I wrote and more, and he has been my most definite rock since we met. Over a decade later, I cannot fault my now-husband for his patience with me and the things that happen in my life that affect him also. He's supported me and *never* doubted me. Sure, we've had to learn how to best communicate with each other and what the other's needs are, as with any relationship, but he helped me take my wall down, brick by brick. We can read each other like a book, and I can't express how grateful I am for him being in my life each and every day.

My mental wellness journey continued seriously over the next few years until I reached a point in my early twenties when I realised how far I had come and no longer identified myself with having mental ill-health. Anxiety was by far the hardest battle because it was so reinforced by many factors, and I didn't truly feel in control of that until a few years later. I didn't feel the baseline anxious feeling any more, but I could still randomly have a panic attack. This just led me to needing strategies that allowed me to keep constantly checking in with myself, as you check in with loved ones and friends. Self-care became an *essential* part of my life, so that I made sure I was looking after myself and not holding things in or doing too much. I assessed the balance of every aspect of life that was important to me and how much energy was going into it. I focused on building my self-esteem, sense of self-worth, self-belief, self-trust, and self-love through my passion for spirituality and psychology. I've healed and overcome so much – we must if we are to truly enjoy life, after all.

While I was studying undergraduate psychology, I was led to volunteer and use all I had learnt so far to help others whose situation I could empathise with. I continued with personal development, growing my self-esteem and altering the landscape of my mind to be a more supportive, helpful, and genuinely beautiful place. I took accountability for things that had happened. That didn't mean that I blamed myself or saw other people as bad, just that I reflected until I understood how I could prevent similar situations from happening in future, and learn the lessons from the experiences. There is no excuse for actions that harm other people, but it did mean that I learnt to see other people with compassion, because they did have their own internal battles, and for whatever reasons weren't handling them well or with any sense of grace.

I eventually gained employment where I was volunteering so I could leave my paid job elsewhere. I continued to work there throughout undergrad and into a psychology master's course. My manager at the charity was more of a mentor, and she encouraged me to pursue counselling because of the great rapport I had with the clients, and because of the skills I was using. I was finishing my master's research project at the time, and looking at prisons to apply to work in, which would have been a totally different career trajectory. Our conversation that day lingered with me, and the more counselling started to feel right. Curiosity led me to look up local courses, and everything was so easy – there was no resistance from the Universe with it at all; I knew it was right.

Cast yourself – you are the spell. – T. Thorn Coyle

Two years into my counselling training, an unfortunate virus led me to partially lose my vision. Thankfully, it fully healed within a few months and miraculously left no damage, but until we knew why my sight was decreasing and before it started to improve, it was the scariest time of my life. I'd not long bought a house with my then-fiancé, and we had booked our first cruise now that I wasn't afraid of ships anymore (or rather, a fear of open water and being stranded at sea)! I felt as though I had everything to live for and couldn't understand why this was happening.

The optometrists told me to go on the holiday and de-stress to give my body a chance to rest because there wasn't anything they could do to help me. With little choice, I did what they said. I had been doing too much as usual: trying to fit friends and family in with work, volunteering, renovating, studying, attending college, hobbies, and navigating a different stage of my relationships with loved ones. Going on that holiday *was* what I needed to re-evaluate everything. I was happy, yet I wasn't, because the balance of my life was totally off again. While I had attention going in all the directions I wanted, too much energy was being given – energy I didn't have, and I burnt out. Boundaries had slipped and needed to be put back in place because I was now pouring from an empty cup, and if I wanted any chance of my eyes healing, I needed to up my self-care big time.

After this holiday, the tension between me and a loved one soon hit a peak. I did a lot more Shadow Work, inner-child work, worked with chakras, used tarot *a lot* and saw a counsellor myself. I realised that it felt even worse between us because each unsatisfactory interaction seemed as though it justified how bad I felt inside and cemented the belief I thought I had healed – that I really wasn't worthy of love. I had healed the parts of me that believed I wasn't worthy of *romantic* love or *self-love*, but not the little girl who wanted to be loved by her *family*, and this came from a few different directions.

I was caught in a negative cycle, trying to please so that I could feel worthy of love, but never being able to meet expectations, because I wasn't being authentic to myself. I was allowing others to treat me poorly, as I wasn't respecting myself within this particular area. It was the one area I was not assertive in. All I had to do was see them wholly through love, communicate with love, and my spirituality helped me to do this like nothing else could. Like *alohomora,* (a spell in the beloved *Wizarding World* of J. K. Rowling) it unlocks you from any negativity, resentment, unfulfilled dreams, etc. Accepting that self-worth is in your soul because you exist, expressing itself through your talents, abilities and experience (just as we unconditionally love a baby or pet companion – because they exist, not because of what they've done or could do). I can't convey how different my relationships are now with family, and how they have done a complete 180 from me being ready to cut ties forever to what is now very supportive and open.

When we learn to open our hearts, anyone, including the people that drive us crazy, can be our teacher. – Pema Chodron

Two years after the eye issue I qualified, registered as a psychotherapeutic counsellor, applied for a new job with less hours, and set up my private therapy practice with the blessing of my so incredibly supportive and amazing husband. Whilst I would not describe myself as ever having been mentally *ill*, as I was not clinical – I was *technically* functioning – I did have very poor mental health. My view of myself (internal), others (external) and the world (global) was negative, hostile at times, and warped. I was not going to be satisfied by dealing with the immediate issues – sorting my thoughts and actions out. I needed to understand *why* these things had occurred, what was going on psychologically, neurochemically, physiologically and on a spiritual/esoteric level, and truly understand my life. I have been on a deep dive to self-understanding and awareness, which has naturally led me down lots of paths, from the empirically scientific, to the philosophical, esoteric, and back to the spiritual.

Now I am using all the very best of what I have learnt personally, from research-based understanding, and from the experiences of my clients over the years to compile this book. Well over a decade later, I look back at this journey and feel peace, because it's what I needed to go through and understand so that I can be the version of myself that I am today, and to do what I do now. It pushed me and allowed me to grow more than sheer curiosity and will to help others could have.

Today, I support others with their own mental health and life issues to arrive at mental wellness and live more authentically, which we can do when we understand ourselves with compassion. I truly believe you can live with mental wellness and all the beauty it brings – creativity, hope, optimism, patience, open-mindedness, compassion, focus, passion … And I am here to support you on *your* journey, using all the skills, knowledge, and wisdom I have acquired. I really hope this book serves you on your own wellness journey and that you find a joyful balance in life that truly works for you.

You are never too old to set another goal or to dream a new dream.
– C. S. Lewis

3 ~ PREPARATION

Each morning we are born again. What we do today matters most.
– Buddah

Before we begin to do any of 'the work' or make changes, there are a few things magickal readers may wish to consider firstly and throughout each following chapter.

Ask for Support

There is strength in asking for support in this journey from those whom you can earnestly trust. Let them know that you're consciously working on trying to improve your sense of wellness or whatever it is you're personally focusing on, and let them know how they might support you with that. Maybe you ask them to hold you accountable to certain things, such as habits you want to build up. Perhaps you ask them to be straight-talking with you so that they don't allow you to make excuses, or they call out your ego. Give them permission for what they can say to you; agree it in writing if you feel that would help! You may even choose to ask someone else to walk on this journey with you and be each other's support buddy. Either way, don't walk alone if you don't have to; things are usually a lot easier with the right support from the right people around you. Don't be afraid to ask for support or whatever you need – if you don't ask, the answer is always no, but if you ask, it might be a yes.

Guides

Ask for support from your spirit team, or from the Universe in general. Throughout each section, you may wish to reflect on which being could support you with your aims. This could include specific deities to help strengthen certain traits you hold or would like to hold, to help banish or diminish something, or simply a deity you ask for general support and guidance.

You may also consider totem animals, angels, or ancestors. Whatever feels right for you. If you don't already work with any guides, now would be a good time to invite them in. There are ways you can connect, such as by following guided meditations, or you can simply ask aloud for a guide to be present with you on this journey, and if you like, ask that they make themselves known to you. You may agree a sign, such as being gifted with a white feather or some other symbol that is personal to you.

Altars

Creating a sacred space is an important part of intention setting for many neo-Pagans, Wiccans, witches, spiritual people, and as a tradition within some other religions. It is a particular space dedicated to your highest good and as a focus for your current intentions. Many people also choose to include representations of the elements on there, and symbolism or imagery that represents any beings worked with. For me, it's my go-to place for peace. It is where I do most of my magical working, meditation, divination, reflection, and journaling. I connect there with my intentions, the elements, power animals, deities, Higher Self, and Spirit in general. This should be a space that inspires you and fills you with emotions you want to feel, such as peaceful, loving, centred, grounded, connected. It can be a whole room if you like, or a shelf or something you put away and pull out when you need it.

Spells and Rituals

A spell is simply a prayer with props, and the consideration of which props to use allows you to go deeper into your intention for the spell, which will be the outcome that you would like to achieve with said spell. Intention is very important during spells, and you must be aligned with your intent for them to be effective. This going deeper allows you more clarity and more personalisation, which should help spell work to feel more powerful. Psychologically, this embeds the intention more into your subconscious. I won't go into the theories of magick here – they've been written about well elsewhere if you're curious to dive into that rabbit hole!

While spells can be as simple as chanting a rhyme, tying knots, or blowing out candles, rituals are usually more elaborate and would use something for each element or each basic sense (sight, smell, taste, touch, hearing) which would be incorporated into the working (carrying out, conducting) of the ritual, although not always. Rituals are also performed as celebrations to mark specific points in time or milestones, and can simply be an act that you perform regularly or habitually, such as morning, evening, Moon or various annual and anniversary rituals. Either way, performing a ritual is a dedicated moment of time that creates a pause in amongst daily life, that feels very grounding yet expansive in how you are often left feeling connected to your life, and what is important in it for you.

Once the working of a spell or ritual is completed, the idea is to take inspired action so that you help to make your intention a reality, with the magickal boost from the spell. Because we live in a material world – we are physical beings made from matter – visualisation alone is not always enough; we also are required to take physical action, otherwise known as inspired action. Some like to think of the magick as giving them a little 'one up,' boosting or tipping the scale in their favour, so long as it is actually meant for them (it's in their highest good for the outcome to be so).

Inspired action is you saying to the Universe, (or whomever you dedicated your working to), 'Hey, I really would like this outcome/manifestation, and I'm willing to do my part to meet this reality; I'm active because I care about this, thank you.' We co-create with the Universe, for it is a creative space, and inspired action helps us meet it halfway. We don't have to go overboard and control every little detail, squashing out the chance of something better, but nor do we sit on our laurels or ask and expect to get automatically. An example being if you really want a new job, you ask for the Universe's support with the spell to make it so for your highest good. Perhaps you bless your CV/resume, but if you don't update it or actually apply for jobs, it doesn't seem like you're serious about wanting this change. If you do what is practically possible, let people know you're looking, apply for jobs etc., you may find a great opportunity presents itself to you that you hadn't considered before! You've raised your game, and because you're being active, you're more likely to notice opportunities and they're more likely to notice you.

Spells are typically ended with the caveat of 'It harm none, so mote it be', or 'May this be for my highest good and the good of all concerned' because we're human (fallible). We can be short-sighted or simply unaware of something better, so this shows our humility – that we're open to better possibilities than we foresaw with the original spell.

Disposing of Used Spell and Ritual Components

After certain magickal workings, you can have things that are the discards and things that cannot be used again. Always be conscious of how and where you dispose of these things once their purpose is spent. Recycle where possible, but if your working calls for you to bury something, then please ensure you only bury that which will naturally biodegrade (such as food and paper), so that it doesn't harm any wildlife, pets, or children if they happen upon it. If you are burying something with the intention to dig it up at a later date, it's better to place it in a glass jar or similar vessel, and then bury it somewhere it won't be disturbed, so it isn't likely to shatter. There's no rule against discarding spell leftovers in the bin; it's better to do that than flush them down the toilet – toilets are not rubbish disposals and can get blocked – and be careful to let ash fully extinguish and cool before moving it, lest it ignite or melt something where it is disposed.

Consecrating

To consecrate is to make sacred, so you may wish to consecrate certain objects or tools that you would like to house on your altar. This act dedicates a tool to your journey and its purpose and attunes it to your personal energy. It also blesses the object by cleansing it with each element and affirms to it its purpose in how it can assist you in your journey. You may like to prepare by writing your own incantations, as whatever you make meaningful to you will be all the more powerful. For illustrative purposes, I have included a very basic example below.

Begin by thinking about how you would like to cleanse your chosen object with each element. Think outside the box. If you have no 'things', then you always have nature around you, including the Sun, which could be used to purify with the element of Fire. Then consider what each element would mean to that object. For example, if I were consecrating a pen and wanted to use only that pen in a book I had dedicated to spiritual or personal development, I might see the role of Fire to be illuminating truth and understanding. Similarly, the role of Air may be to assist me with increasing my comprehension of concepts, Earth to be supporting me with growth and the implementation of new ideas, Water to help me process through emotions healthily, and Spirit's role to be to help me be more of who I truly am and understand the wisdom of my Higher Self.

Once you have clarity on what each element can mean to the purpose of the object to be consecrated, gather the items you need and hold your object as you incant:

'I cleanse and bless this [object name] *by the element of Air so that it might* [declare how this element can empower the object].'

Proceed to introduce the object to your chosen representative for Air. This could mean selecting a particular incense that aligns with your purpose and gently wafting the object in the smoke for a few seconds, or softly blowing on the object with your breath. Then repeat for the remaining four elements.

For Spirit, you may simply like to hold the object and imagine it connecting with you on an energetic level as you say your incantation. You can then use your object and house it on your altar or sacred space when not in use, if that feels right for you. Repeat this ritual as necessary.

You don't need to have anything fancy if you want to do this process. Cleansing with water is called asperging, and water is easy to obtain, but then if you want to go that extra mile with it, you could make Moon or crystal water and put it into a spray bottle, create a herb infusion, gather storm or snow water – whatever feels right for you! Ideas for Earth could be rubbing your object with an oil blend made of herbs you selected for your purpose, using salt or charged salt if you desire, laying it on ground leaves or petals from a particular plant, or simply introducing it to some soil from your garden or sand from a favourite place. Or you could simply lay it on a pentacle if that symbol has a connection to Earth for you as it often does in tarot decks.

You can unleash your creativity with magick, and that is part of what makes it so fun! It also means you can make anything totally *you,* and one of the bonuses of witchcraft is that as you explore your relationship to the simple things around you, you learn more about who you *are.*

Dressing and Marking Candles

Many rituals and spells make use of candles, both because they are used in a practical sense but also as a signal to the unconscious mind that the ambience is different to how it appears normally, and so the magickal mindset is called for. A lot of people enjoy them around the home, without lighting them for a specific reason other than to create a pleasant atmosphere or disperse a nice scent around. Depending on your intention within a spell or in lighting the candle, you can further the potency of it by doing what is called 'dressing the candle'. This works best with already unscented candles, but you can use a particular essential oil or oil blend to enhance the purpose of the ritual; for example, a few drops of a banishing oil could be applied onto the candle during a releasing or cleansing ritual. There's lots of information out there for how you can make oils, and I include some in the resources section at the end of this book.

Additionally, you can inscribe the candle with words or symbols that match your spell. A simple guide is to write or draw clockwise and down the candle when you are bringing something *to* you, and anti-clockwise and up the candle (towards the wick tip) when you are banishing something *from* you. It's easy to take a toothpick or sewing needle and write on your 'ordinary' household candles that you have about a room, what you would like them to do within the room, such as 'cosy', 'safe', 'relaxation', 'fun'. As the candle burns, the oil and inscription add that little bit of extra will into the situation, and hence, extra magick.

You can also draw sigils (see page 165 for sigil creation) and symbols into the wax as well, and if you like, you can mix dried ground or powdered herbs (such as cinnamon or nutmeg) that suit your intent into a little of the oil and rub them over the sigil for extra potency, and especially if you want your design to stand out more.

Think about matching the colour of the candle to your purpose as well. This extends beyond just candles, of course: use colour with intention for pretty much everything! If you already have your own correspondences, then use those, and if you don't, have a think of what each colour represents and means to you personally.

As a starting point if you're stuck you could use:

Pink: affection, beauty, empathy, love, sensitivity, youth.

Red: action, anger, bravery, passion, potency, vitality.

Orange: joy, confidence, courage, creativity, self-esteem.

Yellow: friendship, happiness, inner power, opportunity.

Green: abundance, fertility, freshness, health, self-love.

Blue: calmness, communication, harmony, intellect, peace.

Indigo: business partnerships, intuition, justice, willpower.

Violet: Cosmos, divinity, sovereignty, psyche, spirituality.

Black: divination, overcoming obstacles, protection.

Brown: creatures, comfort, grounding, safety, security.

Gold: luck, money, prosperity, power, success, the Sun.

Silver: intuition, the Moon, serenity, uncovering secrets.

White: all-purpose, clarity, cleanliness, cleansing, purity.

Casting a Circle

The purpose of casting a circle is for it to be a container of energy while you are working magically, and when you are finished, you close the circle and release the energy out into the Universe. Its other important purpose is for it to keep you safe. It is a way of only letting energies you invite into your working space or sacred space. The idea of casting a circle for safety is because practitioners are often ungrounded when their focus is so involved in their intention with their ritual or spell, and they may otherwise be vulnerable to energies (or entities if you prefer to look at it that way) which are not for their highest good. The circle is an ethereal shield.

A circle can be cast by walking in a clockwise direction (or turning on the spot) with your power arm (with the hand you write with) outstretched and pointing your finger or holding a wand or athame, and invoking each element as you face its cardinal direction in turn, and asking the element or guardians of the element for protection, and to assist with your working within the circle. You can also ask them to bring particular traits that relate to them to aid with the working you're doing inside the circle.

There are as many ways to cast a circle as there are practitioners. Each person has their own way, but everyone is respectful, asking the element or guardians for their assistance, not commanding. Some people may call upon their guides to draw the circle and others may ask the Archangels to create a shield around them. Others still may imagine a bubble of light forming around them from light rising up from the Earth and down from the Cosmos. However you chose to form a circle, it should be aligned with what you feel is true for you. I do it differently oftentimes, and sometimes imagine different colours, depending on the purpose of the circle (for example, green for healing and love, rainbow for protection) and have simpler forms and more elaborate forms depending on the reason I want the circle for – it all depends. As with most everything to do with magick, it is down to you as the individual; follow your intuition and you should not stray far. I encourage you to experiment – that is part of the fun!

Timing with the Moon

Working within the Moon phases can be a wonderful way to structure your progress and get into a flow with magick. As with the Gregorian calendar system that we use to chunk the 365-day year into months, the Moon can be used similarly to structure your life further into 28-day cycles. This is not only useful; it also adds an extra layer of magick and meaning into your self-development work. The Moon is for everyone, and its phases can be worked alongside to add extra intention, focus, and power into your wellness journey. Part of magick is working alongside nature, and working with the Moon is another way for the principle of the outer reflecting the inner – as above, so below – to manifest.

There are four main phases of the Moon:

Waxing: beginnings, building, calling in, creativity, expansion, faith, freshness, growth, hope, learning, manifesting, optimism, planting seeds, positive transformation, strength.

Full: abundance, achievement, celebration, completion, fruition, gratitude, harvest, success, wish-fulfilment.

Waning: cleansing, clearing, diminishing, letting go, making space, releasing, shrinking, slowing, shedding, winding down.

Dark: divination, illuminating the hidden, letting things die away completely, peace, rest, the shadow, unconscious, wisdom.

Which phase you work with will depend on what you are doing or how you choose to see something you are working on. To illustrate how you may work with a Moon cycle for self-love, you may start by working with the waning Moon to diminish hurtful self-talk, dark Moon to conduct Shadow Work or perform divination for insight into your blocks on loving yourself, waxing Moon to increase your self-love, and the full Moon to celebrate yourself.

Oracle and Tarot

A spread is included for each element to further assist you with tapping into the energies of each section. Divination in general is a useful method to help you draw out further wisdom within you, and as a way to enhance your learning and development as you reflect on each card's meaning in relation to its position in a spread. It's useful to note your draws for each spread and journal about what comes up for you with each card, and allow further insight to flow. You then have this to refer back to as a memory jog and to track growth, progress, and your evolution. Tarot and oracle cards are a way to tap into your unconscious mind, as can be many other forms of divination; however, many people enjoy the breadth and depth they can gain with cards, and there's so much choice of decks, you can definitely find something to suit you. They encourage you to be analytical and look at things from an objective and sometimes different perspective – something that as a therapist, I am all about!

BOS's, Journal Prompts and the Benefits of Writing

If you already journal, then you know how very useful writing is as a tool. Journaling can help you tap into your unconscious and so develop more self-awareness, as well as helping you to process through emotions and unlock different ways of solving problems. It's also hugely helpful as a means of recording so that you can reflect, and it acts as a way to have a semi-structured conversation with yourself. Because of these benefits and the general popularity with witches and self-development devotees around journaling, you will find prompts in this book when relevant during an exercise, and also at the end of each elemental section.

Many witches will be familiar with the terms *grimoire*, *Book of Tides*, *Book of Shadows*, and *Book of Mirrors*. A grimoire is a book of spells and information (making what you're reading a grimoire). The Book of Shadows (or BOS as it's affectionately referred to in modern culture) is a type of witch's journal where we record our magical workings, a little like a recipe book, and our own musings on certain subjects that we want to record to look back on. Each book will be completely personal to each witch, and each new BOS that they craft will show the evolution of their path as new things become of interest.

A Book of Tides is a Sea witch's version of the BOS; a Sea witch, in a nutshell, is a witch who works exclusively or mainly with the oceans, rivers, lakes, etc., and heavily with the Water element.

The Book of Mirrors is more specifically a journal dedicated to Shadow Work (discussed in more depth in the Spirit section), where the witch records her journey of diving deeper into her unconscious to build self-awareness and personal growth. We will often record dreams and divination results here to reflect on as messages become clearer. The results of spells and rituals will often be recorded here as well so that we can have that record and learn what we may keep the same or do differently next time.

If you're not a pen and paper person and are more of a typing person, then do that instead! The important thing is to be comfortable when you journal – whatever the format. However, if you can, try to handwrite, because the act of writing has been shown to have a calming effect and to help with memory consolidation – two things supportive of wellness.

Note that you may need to limit your time for each question if you have a tendency to dwell on your answer and experience some sort of pain from doing so. Putting a cap on time can keep it the forward-moving, productive exercise that it's intended to be.

The journey of a thousand miles begins with a single step. – Lao Tzu

Working with the Seasons & Wheel of the Year

Whether you are interested in Wicca or not, there is a usefulness to the Wheel of the Year in that it can help you to attune better to the nature around you, and it provides a helpful framework for planning within the usual 12-month calendar year. The Wheel is divided into eight sabbats, which are specific seasonal festivals depending on the position of the Sun in relation to the Earth – the solstices and equinoxes. For the sake of transparency, I worked with the 'traditional' Gardnerian eight sabbats on the Wheel of the Year for many years before I started to truly make them my own. They are each useful for framing the year and can be a great starting point to making your own personal calendar of rituals and celebrations, which is more what I do now as that is more meaningful to me.

The Goddess tradition in Avalon is an example of taking 'traditional' Wicca celebrations and making them your own so that it best reflects your individual views and beliefs. They have specified deities for each of the eight major Sabbats in the year and which directions, elements and other correspondences they believe best represent their primary qualities. They also acknowledge a different cardinal direction system (with North as Air, East as Fire, South as Water and West as Earth), to classical, ceremonial Wicca which views North as Earth, East as Air, South as Fire and West as Water. I also no longer use the ceremonial Wicca direction correspondences because they don't make the most sense for me. I now use North as Air, East as Earth, South as Fire, and West as Water – do what works for you!

One of the whole points of magick and witchcraft is personal development, and part of that is doing what is authentic to you. When things make sense for you, your magick will be all the more potent, because you will have greater faith and trust in what you do. This is one of the reasons I truly believe that witchcraft is an empowering path to be on, and therefore great for wellness. I know that sentiment is shared by many, many witches who've practised The Craft for long enough.

Because this isn't a 'Wicca 101' book, I will briefly explain how you might use the sabbats strategically to assist with building your wellness foundation, or for working generally on your self-development goals, if that is what you chose this book for assistance with. Based on where in the year we are, you may like to start with the corresponding sabbat and suggested section of this book – do what's right for you.

The Wheel of the Year is so called because many cultures have plotted the cycle of the Sun and seasons on a circle and observed that the two solstices and equinoxes divided relatively neatly into four quarters. Wicca halves each of those quarters with another celebration, making the eight sabbats. For each sabbat (and each has several names depending on which Pagan culture is being referred to), you can choose to do further research about it if you're curious, such as its history or role within the modern-day. Regardless, consider the dates it falls on and what that time of year means to you, the feelings you associate with it and the types of activities you often find yourself partaking in around then, as well as what you feel called to in terms of listening to your needs at that time. Ask yourself what colours, scents, flavours, textures and sounds echo that time of year to you.

The general flow between the sabbats is a plant-tend-grow-harvest-till-rest cycle, and that is the basis for how each can support you magickally as you tap into the energies already flowing at that time of year. You'll notice most of the time is spent tending and growing … is it any wonder? Time and energy are crucial for effort, and if we want sweet fruits from our labours of love. Working with natural cycles teaches us on a deeper level that everything is part of the life-death-rebirth cycle, and aids mental health because you understand the importance of growing, shedding the old and evolving yourself and your life. Witchcraft encourages us to face the light and the dark with strength, grace, and compassion, making us better versions of our self.

Imbolc (2nd February)**:** *Plant:* After the rest time of Yule, Imbolc reminds us that as long as the winter may feel, it does not last forever, as spring is around the corner. It's here to ensure that you have made room for growth in your life and cleared out the weeds of your mind that were holding you back so that the beautiful flowers you're planting can blossom. Does your schedule allow what you want to come into it? Assess whether you have what's necessary in place to support and sustain the changes you want to make. If you started anything new in January, assess what is and isn't working for you as well. How can you keep any good momentum already gained, going?

Plant the seeds now for the changes that you want to make, whether that is changes in your thinking, behaviours, or aspects of your life. Do you have a main area of focus this year? If this is the same as last year, and you didn't progress much, consider honestly why that is the case – have you a block on progression, not a solid enough plan, or are you taking on too much? Is a part of you afraid of change or success in this area or actually happy where you are, and why? Is it really your aspiration, or someone else's? Drop resolutions you honestly don't really need and focus more on one thing at a time if you need to, especially if you're tempted to make too many changes at once, as it's hard to sustain them.

Consider what you want more and less of in your life, and ensure that you have not made yourself so busy with goals that you have not left room for joy and rest. Take time to reflect on your inspirations and make preparations so that these are obvious and accessible to you so that if you find your motivation waning, you can be reignited with inspiration. Take the first steps. As with the blossoming of plants, growth first happens below the surface. This thoughtful time lends itself well to the Air element and Air chapter of this book.

Vernal Equinox/Ostara (March 20th-22nd): *Tend*: Spring equinox is a day of balance, where day and night are equal before the days grow longer than the nights again. By now, we are seeing the evidence of buds and new shoots in nature, reflecting to us the fruitful potential of our efforts. If you have been showing up to your goals, you may similarly be noticing some positivity from the changes that you have been making and should feel as though things are picking up pace and progressing nicely. Assess and review now what is going well and not so well, and re-evaluate your goals and strategies.

Make room for continued growth as necessary, which can involve decluttering, cleansing, and cleaning not only our physical environment but our internal one too. Plan and switch to your summer morning and evening routines to make the most of the increasing light and diminishing dark. Certainly then, this time lends itself to Earth and the Earth chapter.

Beltane (1st May): *Tend*: Here the Earth is in her full, abundant and fertile glory – showing us the potent potential of our efforts. Focus on exchanging energy through connection. Run what you're doing by trustworthy others, and get them involved in the process. Get feedback from others, and reflect yourself on what you're happy with and how each goal is going.

Assess your relationship with yourself – how are you speaking to yourself, and are you building your relationship with your intuition? May is a great time for a self-love focus; and as it is connected with relationships and emotions, it's a good time to look at the Water chapter of this book as a starting point if you like.

Summer Solstice/Litha (21st June): *Grow*: The longest day and shortest night of the year, where the time between sunrise and sunset is the longest of the year. June and July, with their long days, are great months for focusing on joy and being really aware of its presence in your life – checking that what you are doing and following is lifting and lighting you up.

Many of us embrace the warmth this time of year and if this is you, make time to relish it as much as possible. Are you having fun in your life and with your evolution? Evaluate what isn't good and rework it. Check in with your vibration and energy. Ensure you're not taking on too much or trying to rush anything – don't burn out. Naturally, it's a great time to have a look at the Fire chapter, get into your passions, and take inspired actions.

Lughnasadh/Lammas (1st August): *Grow*: This is the last celebration of summer, and although in the Northern Hemisphere the days and nights are comparatively warm, sunset comes noticeably sooner. Enjoy summer and her bounty while it's still here. Reflect on what is working and express gratitude for that. Check in with your goals; are you achieving the results you want? Do you need to modify anything? Reassess and refine your strategy for the rest of the year. Most things may feel at their peak, and it's common to be very busy this time of year, as motivation tends to be very high both from the energies and the momentum gained through progress. Therefore, either the Water or Fire chapter would be a good place to start from, depending on your present needs.

Autumn Equinox/Mabon (September 21st-23rd): *Harvest*: At this time of balance, when day and night are equal, assess what has been going well for you. Now is the time to think about what you have already accomplished and experienced so far through the year, give thanks for it, and have it sustain you through the rest of the cycle. What are your strengths and what new skills have you developed over the year? And because it's balance, what has not gone so well – is it still important and does it need re-strategising?

This is a time to amplify your focus on gratitude, especially if you are not doing so already. It's also a time for re-clearing, decluttering, and cleansing our lives as we gather around us that which is important for the approaching winter. In the Northern Hemisphere, switch to your winter night and morning routines, which maximise on the decreasing light and increasing dark from this point forward. The energies here resonate particularly well with starting at the Earth chapter.

Samhain (31st October): *Till*: We begin to truly embark more on the inward, introspective journey again, as all the outward expression of summer's abundance is over for now in nature. The leaves are leaving the trees, after their magnificent colour changes, and entering hibernation. As the trees let their leaves go, you too can release anything that is not working, including old belief systems that no longer serve you. As we acknowledge that everything in nature dies to be reborn somehow in the cycle of life, we show honour to our ancestors, who are the reason we are here today, and other passed loved ones (human or animal).

Now is also the time to let go of our past. If there's anything you're clinging onto that has ended, ask yourself what you need to do in order to release it – and do it. What other drains on your energy and time do you need to cut out before Yule? You may wish to find these things out from Shadow Work if it is not something you do regularly throughout the year. Set your aspirations for the year ahead, including how you want to feel. Make room for this future by clearing out what is not in alignment with your vision. I believe that either the Air or Spirit section can be a good place to start if you are here on the Wheel of the Year right now.

Winter Solstice/Yule (21st December): *Rest*: Leading up to Yule (the shortest day and longest night of the year) is a time to recuperate and enjoy the fruits of your labours, and get set to make your environment as cosy as possible for the dark and cold half of the year. Celebrate and express gratitude for what you have achieved and how you have grown within the last year. Self-care is of particular focus right now as you ensure that you are going into the next cycle with refreshed vigour and clarity.

After Yule, reflect on the year as a whole and contemplate what your priorities are for the next cycle: what is now important to you overall, and where would you like your focus to be? What mistakes can you learn from, and how can you vary your approach moving forwards? Consider how you may expand your comfort zone next year and what may have held you back this year. Be clear on your goals and plan out how you will reach them.

Refine your morning and evening routines for the rest of winter. It's a time of scheduling so that we ensure we make the most of the coming year so that we can look back on it next Yule and be proud of where we are. The big-picture nature of this time lends itself well to the energies of Spirit, and so it's a good time to look at the Spirit chapter of this book.

This breakdown is more appropriate to the Northern Hemisphere; if you are in the Southern Hemisphere, the reverse will be more true for you. There will be calendars and charts online to help you find what is accurate to where you are geographically if you want assistance.

You don't have to see the whole staircase; just take the first step.
– Martin Luther King

Card Spread: Elemental Messages

This card spread is designed to allow you to tap into the messages that each element may have for you at this time. It is working on the poem of 'Earth grows, Water flows, Air knows, Fire glows, and Spirit knows.' Earth is our foundation, and so is that which we grow from; Water is our ever-flowing emotions; Air is our thinking space; Fire is our passion and courage; Spirit is the deep inner knowing of our soul and intuition, and so is wise even if our stomach, head, heart and feet are not. It is also in the flow of a spiral, which shows that we are always on a continuous journey with ourselves.

1. Earth: What messages about my personal growth does Earth have for me right now?

2. Water: What emotions is this element wishing to draw my attention towards at present?

3. Air: What information is this element wanting me to be mindful of at the moment?

4. Fire: What actions would this element like to make me aware of moving forward?

5. Spirit: What does Spirit want me to know right now as I embark on this journey?

If you haven't done a card reading before then as you shuffle the deck, quieten your mind and focus on the spread in question and having the right card for each position, for you.

Open yourself up to the wisdom and be willing to receive. You may find some of the suggestions from page 137 helpful in creating an environment conductive to connecting with your cards and the intention to receive guidance and insights through using them.

Always remember to fall asleep with a dream and wake up with a purpose. - Unknown

Earth

I reap
what I
intentionally
sow

4: EARTH ~ PART I
AS ABOVE

Today I honour my body, I speak kindly to and about it, I listen to what it is telling me and I give it what it needs.

***

Earth is the physical. That which surrounds you in the material world, including your living space, possessions, finances, domestic life, health and body – the vessel for your spirit. Earth is your stability in life and is liked to your sense of stability and connection to the Earth and its flora and fauna. It's considered the slowest-paced element and is associated with delta brain waves, which are released during deep healing sleep. This section is to help you address lifestyle choices that no longer serve your highest good. Creating and beginning to implement new habits that do serve you well and set you up to have the best of days possible.

Connecting with Earth

Take a few moments to pause to consider what the element Earth means to you. Journal your responses to gain more clarity on this. Do you currently feel connected to Earth, and what makes you say yes or no?

Where are your favourite places on Earth?

What life areas linked to the Earth element jump out at you as needing attention?

If you were to personify the element of Earth, what would this character be like?

How would they make you feel in their presence?

Is there anything in this character that you would like more or less of within yourself?

How do you connect with the Earth in your life?

What actions do you take to support our Earth as it surely supports you?

If you haven't already tried the earthing technique described later in this chapter, now would be a good time to try it out. It's an obvious one, but getting outside actually in nature and observing it has a whole field behind it – ecopsychology or ecotherapy – because its benefits are so multifold and clear.

Getting out in nature doesn't have to be to remote, quiet places; it can be a lively park or beach. You don't have to just be passive there; you can take a nature-spotting or foraging walk, cycle, read, draw, paint, stitch, write, picnic, do yoga or tai chi! Whatever takes your fancy.

One of the simplest ways nature helps is it often takes us away from the sources of stress in our lives, it creates a physical distance, and sometimes a psychological distance. It gives space to breathe and can help problems get into perspective and stop being so mountainous. They say a change is as good as a rest, and sometimes that's very true! Changing your scenery can be freeing, so I encourage you not to overlook this one and research the benefits yourself.

Another easy way for anyone, of course, is to grow more plants, especially from seed. Great ones in particular are herbs because they can be used nutritionally and magickally. Nurturing plants is good for promoting feelings of wellness and relaxation, so see what you can do either in a garden, or a pot on a windowsill is just as good. Additionally, it goes without saying but never litter, and further your good by picking up litter you see, recycling correctly and being as eco-friendly as you are able to be.

An Analogy for Understanding Energy – Your Teapot

A good method of understanding your energy, or lack thereof which is known as fatigue, is with the teapot. Imagine you are a teapot. The teapot is you, and the teacup is your life. There may be other teacups at the service, and these are other people. Each night, the lid comes off, and the teapot filled up with four types of energy, or ingredients in this analogy: a *teabag* (physical energy), *water* (emotional energy), *milk* (mental energy), and *sugar* (spiritual energy).

The teabag represents the energy we get from sleeping well, from your body absorbing the nutrients from your food, from being hydrated, and from your body being physically well and recovered. It is the foundation that affects the others (it's just hot watery milk without the tea)! If this is lacking, then the others will suffer as well because the quantity of energy is lacking. If the teabag is tiny, or you've only had it in your pot for a few seconds, then the brew will be weak indeed! It is affected by the nutritional value of the food you eat, the quality of sleep you have, and the exercise you get. Your body really is a temple that houses your soul or Self, and so it is what allows you to have a human experience, which is why it is so important to look after and appreciate it.

Water is your emotions, and so it is the energy you receive from how you feel, and it dictates the quality of your energy. It affects how you interact with others and your performance – what you put out into the world. If you're full of negativity and gloom, if your mind is stressed and cluttered, you will have a low-vibe energy and likely have little patience with others. Your water would be muddy coloured. Eurgh! No one wants a drink made with murky water! It is also how clear you are on your feelings, and the extent to which the feelings you're aware of are your own, or if emotions from other people are clouding your own.

Milk is your mental energy and pertains to cognitive functions. It relates to your ability to focus your attention, organise and understand your thoughts, manage your emotions, exercise your will, and make decisions and choices. If you're burnt out, then it's harder to make choices that will be better for you in the long run, and your reactions to things can be high or low, proportional or disproportional. We'll be more likely to look for short-term fixes and become lazy in our efforts. Your milk will be sour, and you won't be able to think clearly, or may not be bothered to spend time thinking things through if your mental energy is lacking.

Sugar is the sweet stuff. It's you in your uniqueness, in *your* life. Spiritual energy comes from living authentically, doing activities that feel essential to who you are, following your purpose, finding meaning and being congruent. It reflects your core values and is your less discernible 'senses': sense of direction within life, sense of belonging and connection with others, etc. It's also your sense of the bigger picture for yourself and is what you're aware of in the background of your day-to-day life. In essence, it can feel like motivation and inspiration.

If all of your ingredients are balanced and replenished, then your teapot will be full of a delicious brew that's totally unique to you! Your lid will go on when you wake up, and you'll awaken feeling refreshed, happy, focused and motivated. You'll pour that brew into your teacup first, and that will be the energy you're working with for that day. If you're managing your energy really well and life is pretty calm, you should have extra brew in the pot that keeps your cup topped up throughout the day.

This 'overflow' is what is referred to when people say 'fill your own cup up first and live from the overflow'. You have more than enough for your needs, so you have the capacity to share of yourself generously with others. If the demands of the day are more than the energy you have and there is nothing left in the pot, then you risk burnout. You're using energy that you don't have, and you can become unwell, or at least very fatigued and grumpy.

As you go through your day, you'll be required to use some of the energy from your cup. Sometimes you'll replenish it with different activities depending on which energy type needs topping up. For example, if it's physical, then resting or a smoothie may help; for emotional, it may be getting a cuddle (if water's low) or exercise (if you need to clear the water up a bit); for mental, it may be meditation or taking a break; for spiritual, it may be some journaling to realign yourself, or a walk somewhere inspiring.

Some restorative activities may replenish more than one ingredient, and they may become part of a daily wellness and self-care habit or routine for you. Passions often fulfil at least two energy types, which is why they mean more than simple interests or preferences.

Perhaps by the end of the day, you're ready for sleep, but you aren't exhausted, you're not *drained,* just looking forward to a full rest. When you understand your teapot and its contents, you don't let the ingredients expire – you don't run on empty – you care not to let yourself get to that point; you know what's good for your wellness.

However, if you're not well – perhaps you're fighting an illness, not handling stress well, not practising self-care, criticising yourself unfairly, feeling guilt or shame, not standing up for yourself, becoming overwhelmed by responsibility or emotions, not eating well or regularly enough or perhaps too much and feeling sluggish, drinking too much of the wrong thing, sleeping poorly, making poor decisions or rash judgements – how would your teapot and brew be? It'd drain very fast, probably not fill up much in the first place, and not be very nice tasting. I'd imagine the pot and cup would also start to look a little worse for wear too. When your teapot's relatively empty, it's harder to make the right decisions and choices for you. That's why you pick something and start there: do what you can, with what you have, when you can.

Note that your brew will not necessarily look the same as anyone else's. Your cup of tea is not everyone's, and that is okay – you do what works for you. Self-awareness plays a huge role in wellness and therefore, in energy management.

Take a moment now to consider your teapot and brew. Write your responses to the following so that you can reflect back at a later date:

~How full are your cup and pot right now?

~How do you know how full they are?

~What does it all look like if you imagine it in the physical?

~What drains its contents the most?

~Do you know what's important to you in life, and do you truly live like it is?

~What do you do that adds to your teapot daily/weekly?

~Do you savour your blessings and accomplishments?

~What do you need to do to maximise replenishment of your teapot's energy?

~Do you take time to really enjoy an activity or connection that you have with someone else? How often?

~What type of energy do you struggle to replenish?

~Do you tend to rush or neglect replenishing your energy?

~How can you manage your energy more effectively?

~What will you commit to right now and implement?

~If you're creative: Illustrate and colour the teapot, cup and brew as they are now, and the ones you'd like to have.

Self-Care – Topping Your Cup up to Keep it Flowing

Through acts of self-care, you replenish your energy throughout the day, and sometimes this will spill over into the next day, and so on, depending on the activity and what is going on in your life. Self-care is self-love in practice, and together they allow you to present the best version of yourself, at that moment, to the world. So, for each energy type, you can have different methods of self-care, and these can be practical and spiritual practices that make you feel as though your vibration is high.

As previously mentioned, some activities can restore one or more types of energy. You need only find what works for you, and being clear on what does work cannot be underestimated in its value to you for the long-term.

Create a self-care list: write each of the energies out and list under them all the activities that you can do where, after engaging in them, you feel refreshed and recharged (you can include certain spells and rituals here are well). These are the activities that fill your physical, emotional, psychological, and spiritual energies up in the pot, and essentially de-stress you through doing something that is good for you.

I cannot emphasise the importance of this list enough. Use it when you're stuck for an idea of what to do. Some of my favourite daily things are playing with or cuddling my pets, reading a non-fiction book, meditating, having a massage (can be a self-given hand massage, it doesn't need to be at a full-blown spa unless you want to) or reiki session, taking a bath, doing some mindful colouring or crafting, watching a comedy show or favourite film, pottering in my garden, and having a dance around and a sing-along to my favourite uplifting songs. Add this list to your self-love/wellness toolbox so you have it to refer back to, and add to as you become aware of new things.

The Foundation of It All - Sleep

A great thing is that sleep can be improved in spite of co-occurring mental health or substance misuse issues, and it is vital to feel well-rested in order to concentrate, have patience, exercise willpower, and learn new skills in addition to all of the physical benefits of sleep. It is one of the body's cycles, and while we may all have a restless night every now and again, caffeine is not a replacement for good sleep. The following are several questions to help you assess what may be holding you back from getting a great night's sleep. In addition to biological science that informs research about sleep, much of the psychology in this area is stimulus control, which is about the psychological connections made between our environment, actions, and feelings.

As you go through each of the points below, take a notebook and write down steps that you need to take in relation to each question. This will give you action points to be well on your way to improving your sleep.

Is your bedroom actually comfortable, quiet, and fit for sleeping in?

I'm a huge advocate of understanding how our environment makes us feel. Do you actually feel restful, peaceful, or sleepy when you step into your bedroom, or do you feel overwhelmed, overstimulated and stressed? Our bedroom should be comfortable, quiet, and you should be able to make it as dark as you can so that no light could be bothering you at night. Many people find that keeping their bedroom tidy and clean helps a lot because it removes unnecessary stimulation from the environment because even though you may not be consciously thinking about picking up that laundry on the floor, your subconscious noted it. Have fun experimenting with your environment and making it and your bed as inviting for sleep as possible. This may involve investing in better quality and hypoallergenic bed linens, mattress, curtains, rugs, mood lighting, calming scents, organisation, bigger bed, eye mask, earplugs, etc.

Are you using your bedroom for things other than sleeping?

If you can, keep your bedroom for just sleeping, dressing, and being physically intimate. This tells your brain and body that when you are in this space, the objective is relaxation and sleep, making it easier to achieve as this connection strengthens over time. If you can, keep your bed for pretty much just sleeping, as your body will associate it with sleep and feel tired as soon as you lie down.

Do you wake in the night either too warm or cold?

Excessively warm or cool environments disturb sleep. There is a certain point during the sleep cycle when our body temperature reaches its lowest (usually about 3 am); if you wake here too cold then maybe a blanket or warmer PJs would help. The research-recommended room temperature for sleeping is 16-18°C / around 65°F.

Have you tried having a hot bath or shower before bed?

When you come out from a hot shower or bath, the heat leaves your skin rapidly to the surrounding air, causing your core temperature to drop which leaves your brain and body to believe that it is time for sleep.

Do you clock watch?

This can definitely lead to stress and frustration. If this is you, simply turn the clock away or omit it from your room entirely.

Are you getting enough sunshine?

If you have problems falling asleep, try to get 30 minutes of natural light during the day, and minimise artificial light during the night. This helps to reset your circadian rhythm (body's natural schedule) and the balance of sleep hormones.

Do you wake in the night to go to the toilet?

Could having your last drink earlier help with this? It may also be psychosomatic (imagined) or due to a medical reason – consult your GP if in doubt.

Do you consume caffeine too soon before bed?

There is caffeine in coffee, tea, energy drinks, colas, and some chocolate, which inhibits the hormone adenosine that is part of your homeostatic drive (biological urge to sleep). The guidelines of when is the best time to last consume caffeine in the day do change periodically and will depend on the time you set for sleep. It is helpful to track this yourself because caffeine does stay in the system for a certain time. Monitor this by noting your wake time in the morning, and the caffeine you have throughout the day and the time you have it. You can then see whether this is affecting your sleep by noting when you managed to fall asleep approximately. I find I can have my last caffeine drink in the summer at 4 pm, and in the darker months, I can extend that to 6 pm. Commit to figuring out your personal relationship with caffeine to find the harmonious point. You may also like to extend this investigation to nicotine (a stimulant) and alcohol as they affect sleep cycles as well, usually by causing awakenings during the night/light sleeping.

Are you eating well?

A healthy diet will of course improve your chance to fall asleep fast and the quality of sleep, so do your research and assess what you may need to consume more or less of to improve your diet. This will involve looking into the vitamins and minerals that affect sleep, and whether you consume them regularly and are able to absorb them into your bloodstream. Avoid heavy eating and sugary things two-four hours before sleep, as this can lead to restlessness, but essentially, it's considered best to avoid being too hungry or too full before bed. It may be worth monitoring this too to see if anything does or does not agree with you and affects your sleep or how tired you feel.

Are you getting any or enough physical exercise?

You may have experienced an occasion where you've had a really active day, and you don't even really remember falling asleep after you lay down … Exercise can lead to deep sleep. and it certainly improves your chance of falling asleep. Avoid strenuous exercise three hours before bed though; otherwise, you may still be too stimulated to sleep (unless you *know* this doesn't affect you adversely). Also note, exercise will affect how you metabolise caffeine.

Do you nap too long in the day?

Napping too long or late in the day can make sleep more difficult at night. Sometimes we have to assess honestly whether it is better to have a 20-40-minute power nap, go to bed earlier, or stick to our designated bedtime. Power naps can work wonders, but actually going to sleep for over an hour can be harmful to sleep hygiene, especially if the nap is later in the day (research suggests after 3 pm). Some people will find it necessary to nap somewhere other than their bed as they cannot *just* nap otherwise. I personally find napping on top of the bed with a blanket over me is sufficient. There is a type of super-nap which involves drinking a caffeine beverage, and straight after, having a nap for under an hour.

Do you have a sound bedtime routine?

This can sound silly to adults as it is something often associated with children; however, it is still a necessary part of us taking responsibility for ourselves and fostering good habits. A pre-sleep routine signals to the brain that it is time to get ready for sleep. It is important to *unwind* at the same time each night and to do your chosen activities in the same order, as it strengthens the message that sleep is coming. Write out your bedtime routine, i.e. have a non-caffeinated drink, prepare your lunch for the next day if you leave for work, load the dishwasher, do five minutes of meditation, do five minutes of gentle yoga, get your outfit ready for tomorrow, brush teeth, read a few chapters of a novel. You should then be going to sleep at the same night each night which will set your biological clock and allow your body to work like … clockwork.

Do you use your screens before bed?

This is problematic due to the blue light affecting the hormone melatonin cycle, which prepares the body chemically for sleep. I find the best practice here is to have a sun-tracker on your devices so that the screen dims and controls the amount of blue light emitted according to the Sun. This reflects then the natural cycle of melatonin, despite the season. Some people will find it necessary to be very strict and turn all screens off at a certain time and keep them out of their bedroom, due to being too emotionally stimulated by whatever they are seeing on their screens. Be honest with yourself here – what do you need to do to maximise your success in sleeping well?

Do you feel safe going to sleep?

If you don't feel totally safe, any feelings of anxiety can surface and make it hard to actually relax. Have an appropriate symbol of safety with you whilst you're in bed, be it a cuddly toy or weighted blanket. Attend to what you can do that lessens any feelings of stress and signals *calm and safety* to your sympathetic nervous system so that the parasympathetic nervous system can take over. Such activities can be reading, a guided meditation, or playing with a zen garden as they give your mind something to focus on, which allows it to calm. Slow and deep breathing while listening to slow-paced music or ASMR videos can also signal calm and induce relaxation. Alternatively, do something that makes you laugh, i.e. watching a comedy, because laughter is the opposite of anxiety. The last thing you'd do if you were concerned for your safety is indulge in laughter as your guard would be down, so this is another way to signal to your body that it is okay – you are okay.

Have you tried visualising whilst you're lying in bed?

Some people find it helpful to imagine themselves in a relaxing location and may even enhance the visualisation with ambient music. You can get specific ambient music or white noise devices that have various timer settings which can replace a traditional alarm clock, or some that have no clock feature. This can also be useful for people with tinnitus or in a noisy location, who do not want to/cannot use earplugs.

Do you struggle to get to sleep due to ruminating on things or a whirring mind?

Plan time earlier in the evening for problem-solving, planning, list-making, etc. If a worry pops up, remind yourself you have already allocated time to work on it and let it go. Refer to the techniques in the Air section of this book for help with this issue. Thinking calmly of all of the things you are *grateful* for and picturing them in your mind's eye is also really helpful for relaxation. You can also *visualise* yourself reaching a goal and go to sleep imagining that is your reality – be it holidaying, being in a fulfilling job, having fun with loved ones, etc.

Have you labelled yourself as an insomniac or simply a person who cannot sleep?

The stories that we tell ourselves and the boxes that we put ourselves in are very powerful because they create a self-fulfilling prophecy. The more you tell yourself you can't sleep, the more difficult it actually is to believe you can sleep, and so the more difficult it actually is *to* sleep. Change your story, even if it doesn't feel true right now – it will be. Challenge the story you're telling yourself, and it becomes easier to change. Look for evidence to the contrary – when was the last time you did sleep well? Have you had a period in life where sleep was easier?

Do you force yourself to sleep?

If you do not fall asleep within 20 minutes of turning out your light, get up and go into another room; otherwise, you can cause more stress to yourself and associate your bed with agitation. Engage in a quiet and calming or boring activity in not-too-bright lighting, such as washing up, reading, drawing, colouring, or writing in a journal until you are sleepy. Repeat if you wake up in the night and do not fall back asleep within 15 minutes.

What is your goal for being in bed and 'going to sleep'?

If you're focusing solely on being asleep and that's not the case, then simply not 'reaching' that goal can be causing you stress. Try making the goal instead to *rest*. Simply lying in bed, feeling cosy and *resting*. This can be achieved by feeling how relaxed your body is, your closed eyes are, and being aware of how nice that is. This can help by taking some of the pressure off to *force* sleep because it can't really be forced, it just comes naturally …

Are you still not feeling tired when you go to bed?

If you do find yourself still struggling to fall asleep, or waking up throughout the night after persisting with the tips above for at least one or two Moon cycles, it may be worth trying a technique called *sleep-restriction*. This involves going to bed at the time you usually fall asleep, even if this is 3 am. Once you have consistent chunks of sleep between, say, 3 am and 8 am (or whenever your wake-up time is), you then extend your bedtime by fifteen minutes, making your new bedtime 2:45

am. This then repeats until your new bedtime is 2:30 am and so on until you have a continuous restful sleep period.

If you've done all of the above and still find yourself lying awake…

Try the progressive muscle relaxation technique. Close your eyes, take several deep breaths, and bring your attention to your face and picture each muscle relaxing. You can tense each muscle first if that helps. Do this slowly with each area of your arms, body and legs. As thoughts pop in your mind, let them pass and bring your attention back to the muscle group you're relaxing and your breath. Repeat each night, and with practice, you will enter the relaxed state quicker and quicker.

Other things to note:

I use a sunlight lamp/alarm for the winter mornings to gradually introduce more light into the room which I find necessary to help me wake up. It also works to set it to sundown, so the light in the bedroom gradually dims and helps reinforce to my brain that it is sleep time.

You will need to monitor to find your own level of sleep to feel rested, e.g. mine is seven to nine hours. Note any medications you use – some contain caffeine or have side effects that affect sleep. If after three weeks of implementing all of these steps and you have not felt an improvement in your sleep and how you feel, then *please* consult your GP/medical practitioner, as there are several medical reasons sleep can be poor, despite your best efforts.

You should now have a rather comprehensive list of action points that you can work through to improve your sleep. It will likely be necessary to do further research or consult other professionals, such as dietitians or a sleep coach if you work changing shift times. It should also be noticed that there is a complex interplay between many of the factors which affect sleep (caffeine, exercise, diet, season), so you will need to tailor everything to your own body's needs.

Many of the points you will need to be really firm with yourself on, and really commit to them for your own wellness. Devise a way to hold yourself accountable, and reward yourself when you achieve an action *consistently* for a set time because it will take a few weeks to know whether something helps you. This also helps to build up good habits around your sleep. Good sleep sets us up for the best success in the day – whatever that looks and feels like to you.

Sometimes the most important thing in a whole day is the rest taken between two deep breaths. – Etty Hillesum

Your Body Is a Temple

Our bodies are incredibly complex systems and consist of many parts working synchronously. Consider how you care for the different parts: skin, gut, liver, stomach, kidneys, lungs, heart, teeth, hair ... Do you know enough to be able to care for them well?

Where can you improve and how?

It goes without saying that exercise is as good for the mind as it is vital for the body. Exercise can be an outlet for stresses, tension, and channelling emotions, and it can be a self-care activity that you do alone or with friends. Recommended exercise levels vary depending on your age, but as long as you are allowing your body sufficient time to recover from exercise between workouts, and listening to your body, so you don't push past your limits, that should ensure that you do not over-do it and cause injury. Always consult with a professional if in doubt or you want specific guidance for your particular circumstances and goals.

Different forms of exercise will have different specific benefits, and certain ones will appeal more than others. Martial arts are a great way to improve physical balance and mental focus and increase confidence. Group dance classes can be fun, uplifting, and allow you to safely express a side of you that perhaps you don't otherwise get much opportunity to. There's synchronised swimming, all manner of team and racket sports, rock-climbing, athletics, strength-based training, yoga, Pilates, outdoor gyms, hiking, scrambling, cycling, roller-skating, and even a good old skipping rope or hula-hoop in your own garden.

Most of us wouldn't deny the benefits of exercise and know that we do actually feel better after having done it. One of the hardest parts with exercise, especially if it involves leaving the house, is actually getting there, or into a frame of mind where you feel ready for it.

As with anything, sometimes you do have to be a bit tough-loving with yourself if you know you're procrastinating for no good reason. There are always reasons not to do something – we need to find and feel the reasons to do the thing. Self-parent yourself and list off all the benefits and reasons to go and do it, and follow them up with an affirmation: '…and because I love myself and respect my body and mind, I will go and do this for my highest good right now.' Ride that momentum off the sofa and out of the front door.

It may also help to prepare any kit or clothing you need the night before and have it ready by the door or in your vehicle. At least you can't procrastinate then by needing to look for certain things, as it will already be ready for you. Alternatively, get into the mood to exercise the way you may have gotten yourself into the mood before a night out, party, or big event. This usually involves putting on upbeat music, having a particular beverage and having fun getting yourself 'dressed up'.

What you do here is set the mood to cultivate the 'party' spirit within yourself. As an introvert, this is something I have done many a time before a busy social event because my natural instinct is to usually stay at home with a book or a craft project!

Use this technique to 'go against' your natural instinct that conflicts with doing your chosen form of exercise. Sit and make a plan of what you can do to get yourself into the mood to exercise.

Consider music, guided meditation, clothing, and actions you can take, such as having a dance around at home first to raise your energy (and heartbeat). Also, contemplate what you may need to have done or ready before so that you aren't tempted to use it as an excuse not to exercise because it 'needs doing.'

Once you have successfully done this and completed the exercise a few times, you'll have cognitive, emotional, and physical evidence that you do enjoy the exercise or class, and you will resist it less.

Consuming Consciously - Food and Nutrition

Certain foods can have mood-boosting qualities, such as those containing serotonin, which is a happiness neurochemical. It is well worth your time getting to understand what you are putting into your body and asking why you are consuming it. You may realise you would be better off eating more or less of a particular food. This is part of understanding yourself and showing yourself love because you come to care about what you consume.

You may wish to work with a nutritionist alongside deepening your understanding of your own personal relationship with different foods and drinks. One thing that is always recommended is ensuring you consume enough water throughout the day. It is vital for ensuring a healthy flow of your digestive system, as well as hydrating your brain, which aids in mental activities. If it helps, get a water bottle you *want* to drink out of, such as the kind you can place water-safe crystals into safely, or diffuse fruit into the water so that it can positively enhance your experience of drinking.

When the roots grow deep, there's no reason to fear the wind.
– African Proverb

EARTH ~ PART II
SO BELOW

Every moment is a fresh beginning. – T. S. Eliot

***

Tea Magick

A lot of witchcraft is contained within the everyday things; it's far less often about the grand and elaborate rituals. Preparing your food and drinks with a little more intention is a simple and everyday way to bring a little magick into your own food and drinks.

You can chant while preparing food, recite affirmations while cooking, or simply inform the food and drink of what you'd like it to bring as you or others consume it. I like to imagine different feelings while I'm pouring tea – that's my favourite way to do this, such as pouring in peace, love, contentment. That way, even if I'm distracted while I drink it, I have already taken the moments to set that intention and give a little boost while I drink.

Stirring is another easy way to boost what you're making. The easiest of which is to stir in a clockwise (deosil/with the Sun) motion if your will is to bring something towards you, and an anticlockwise (widdershins/against the Sun) motion if you want something to move away or dissipate from you. You can stir in the shapes of sigils (see page 165 for creation) or personal symbols that hold power for you, and if you are trained in reiki, you can draw those symbols into your drink and cooking. If you're not much of a hot beverage drinker, you can still do this with a reusable/compostable straw or spoon before you drink or eat.

Once you know a little about the specific nutrition and magickal associations of ingredients such as fruits, berries, herbs, and edible flowers, you can consciously blend these to make your own teas or use them to infuse water (see resources section for recommended books). An easy way to blend tea is to start with a base (green, white, black, oolong or rooibos tea), and add your chosen ingredients, depending on properties or how you feel when you drink them; but, you don't need the tea base if you don't want it, especially if you don't want caffeine at that moment.

Bases have certain properties too:

Black tea: expelling negativity, grounding, protection.

Green tea: abundance, love, self-love, spiritual healing.

Oolong tea: concentration, defence, meditation, reflection.

Rooibos: action, bravery, courage, motivation, willpower.

White tea: beginnings, clarity, energy cleansing, wisdom.

The following are some of my favourite tea blends, which would equate to an equal amount of each ingredient if storing in a jar, but adjust to your specific taste:

Beau-tea *to promote skin health*: apple, burdock, dandelion, lemon balm, raspberry, and strawberry.

Clari-tea *for journaling and problem-solving time*: camomile flowers, lemon verbena/balm, marjoram, mint, rosebuds.

Creativi-tea: cocoa husks, peppermint, roasted chicory root, rosehips, and a dash of agave nectar while brewing.

Hones-tea *for self-compassion*: chicory flowers, fenugreek flowers, marigold flowers, grated orange peel, passion flowers, you can add a dash of agave nectar to your taste.

Immuni-tea: dried hawthorn berries, echinacea flowers, ginger root, lemon (juice, peel, or slice – whatever you prefer), lime blossom, and honey or agave nectar to taste.

Infini-tea *for more chance of lucid-dreaming*: burdock, lavender, lemon balm, mugwort leaves, peppermint, valerian root.

Positivi-tea *for that extra boost*: blackberries, elderberries, spearmint, hibiscus flowers, marigold flowers, rosehips.

Puri-tea *for an internal cleanse*: green tea, lemon verbena, marigold petals, passion flower, and rosehips.

Sensuali-tea *for enhancing self-love*: camomile flowers, cranberries, hibiscus flowers, rose flowers, and vanilla.

Simplici-tea *for when you need a reset*: camomile flowers, blue cornflowers, lemon verbena, sweet vanilla, (this blend works especially well with white tea).

Sereni-tea *for winding down before bed*: camomile, lavender, lime flower, lemon verbena, passion flower, vervain, and oat flowering tops.

Spirituali-tea *for ritual mindset*: ginseng, nasturtium, peppermint, raspberries, and violet.

Stabili-tea *for when you need to ground*: dried/fresh beetroot (small chunks), echinacea root, ginger root, orange peel, and turmeric.

As always, check that each ingredient is safe for *you* to consume as a tea (otherwise known as a tonic) and that it does not cause any contraindications with any other medications that you may be on. Some things are not safe to consume while pregnant or if you have a heart condition so do your research (see the books in the resources chapter at the end of this book) and consult your medical practitioner or a licensed herbologist.

Cultivating Consciously – Your Environment

You may already be aware that your environment has an influence on how you feel. I've always been very aware of this, and there is a lot of research now that supports long-standing anecdotal evidence to the fact. Part of magick is having a balance and sense of harmony with our environment, and that goes for the natural world as well as our personal spaces.

Our homes in particular have a large effect on our mental wellness and our overall happiness, unsurprisingly because they are a place that most of us spend a lot of time within over the course of a week, and they should be a place that we can feel ultimately safe within, able to relax and unwind in and be our real Self. Our home is (should be) a place of restful and restorative sanctuary and comfort, where we let our guard down, take off any masks and connect with our loved ones. Our home should also be a place where we can de-stress and prepare mentally, emotionally, and physically for the next day.

The question is then, is your space actually serving you to the best of its capability? This is about tidying, cleaning, and decluttering your personal spaces, including home, working spaces, and vehicles. The amount of influence you have within a space may be limited for a number of reasons, but where possible, it may be worth considering discussing with other people involved how you can all benefit more from the space you share, and take the lead on this.

First, list out each space you have control over, and then assess how you want to feel in each room or each section of a room: do you feel the way you'd like to in it? How do you want to feel in it, and what is blocking that feeling if it's not present or very strong?

Second, create a sense of space by decluttering and organising. Everything ideally should have a home within your home – if it doesn't, does it really have a purpose with you? What needs to go out of the room so you can have your chosen feelings there?

Third, improve the room and adapt it to your needs – see it as an investment in your happiness. What may you need to change about the room to feel the desired way? Perhaps the room doesn't flow as well as it could – have a look into Feng Shui to see if that can inspire you. What needs to come into the space? Consider the effects of natural light, artificial light, lighting options to alter mood or serve a purpose, art, comfort, practicality, the unhindered movement of people and animals within the space, colour, scent, shapes, layout, the size of things, the tactile experience in a space (material and texture of objects and furnishings), temperature, privacy, storage and organisation.

Fourth, consider how you can create an emotional connection to the space by filling it with things that you love. This could also involve curating displays of inspiration, collections of personal history, family, travel, interests, and memorabilia.

And finally, how can you bring a little of the outside in and give a sense of connection to nature, even though you may be in four walls separating you from nature in many ways? How about plants, natural textures, materials, and nature prints?

Creating and caring for your immediate environment is a great way to learn more about yourself, refine your taste, and express your style and what you love. Putting care and attention into your space means that you're performing an act of self-love because your habitat is an extension of you. You can both serve each other well with a little initial consideration and maintenance.

Physical and Energetic Space Cleansing

There are many ways to refresh and restore a sense of peace, balance, and orderliness to your environment. Regardless of whether you practice energetic cleansing or not, your spaces will need physically cleaning, and there are ways to do so with more intent and witchy purpose. Firstly, I like to ensure that the cleaning products I use are of a high quality (eco-friendly, pet-friendly, cruelty-free, etc.) because then I know they are also more high-vibe, and no part of me feels bad for using them. If in doubt, it's so easy to make your own products and tailor the scents for your purpose, for example, using lavender for calming energies perhaps if your space often feels chaotic or if highly-strung people frequent it, or citrus scents for a more energetic and focused feel. There are many recipes to be found online, and a few of my favourite herbal books which have cleaning recipes in are in the resources section at the back of this book.

When in the physical act of cleaning, I like to clean in a counter-clockwise direction and intone what I am cleaning away, then clean over the area or room in a clockwise motion and intone what I am wishing the space be filled with – what energies I want to attract. It's amazing the extra boost this gives to your space, and you may also notice a difference within people and animals who occupy the space too.

You can also chant while vacuuming. I love this one, especially after heavy energy has filled the area, perhaps from someone releasing a lot of emotion. Imagine the vacuum is sucking up more than just dirt and dust, and chant something like, 'Clean this room, clean this space, suck stale energy up, leave positivity in its place.' As a side note, if you're shy about chanting, doing so while vacuuming is an ideal place to start as most vacuums are pretty loud so unless you shout, you're unlikely to be heard.

Cleansing space energetically can be done at any point when the space is physically clean and tidy but may still feel like it needs a shift. Perhaps the purpose of the space has changed, and it's no longer reflecting the 'vibe' that you want. Maybe an argument had occurred there, a difficult event, or simply someone visiting had left a heavy energy there.

Think of your senses and how you may use each one to clear the space and invite what you'd like in – decide what would work for you and for the space you're cleansing. Whether you use a scent from an incense, herb bundle, spray to asperge, or oil burner, you can use a feather fan or your hand to gently waft the smoke or mist around the room, walking first anticlockwise and then clockwise, chanting whatever suits your purpose. It's normal to have the windows open if you can, so the 'negativity' has somewhere to exit. I usually envision it being pushed out by the smoke to be neutralised by the Earth and Air outside. Do what feels right to you. There's no right or wrong with spirituality and witchcraft, so long as you're observing health and safety and not putting yourself or anyone else at risk of harm.

Sound is a really easy way to cleanse. All that noise you make at New Year's – that's a way to shake off the energy of the old year and welcome in the new, and some traditions believe that it helps to ward off any nefarious spirits that may have been lingering around; that ruckus you make is thought to scare them off. Use bells, gongs, singing bowls, anything that is small enough for you to carry around a room in the same fashion as described above, and that is also a pleasant sound to you. If you don't have anything like that, then you can always try music of a particular instrument or simply a song that feels like a reset when you play it pretty loud. If you do that, you can also meditate in the middle of the room and imagine the sound waves pushing out the old energy and replacing it with new. This is particularly good if you aren't comfortable with or able to perform any of the cleansing methods mentioned above.

Another method is to sweep with a besom, which is a usually handmade wooden broom, used specifically for magickal purposes and not actually for sweeping dirt. You would use it in the same manner as with wafting smoke but you 'sweep' the air. Again, you can combine this with chanting, a scent, and music as well.

If your space feels like it *really* needs a huge shift in energy, why not use all five elements in some form. Steady yourself first and be clear on what you're going to chant. What you chant represents Spirit because it is your will and intent. Sprinkle some blessed salt in each corner of the room going in an anticlockwise direction, which represents Earth. Return to the centre and light a scented candle in a colour of your choice (I'd choose white for cleansing). Whilst looking into the candle flame, say your chant either a set number of times if you favour numerology, or until you feel it's time to stop. As you do so, see in your mind's eye the salt absorbing the unwanted energy.

Light your chosen scent of incense or herb bundle and walk around the room anticlockwise wafting the smoke, continuing your chant and envisioning the undesired energy leaving the space. Do so a set number of times (I like three because it's a power number for me) or until you feel the energy has shifted. Set your incense down safely if it's still burning and pick up a spray bottle of charged water. In a clockwise motion, spritz this in the four corners of the room and return to the centre. Shut any windows you may have opened and collect the salt back up. You may bury this in a little hole in the garden or dispose of it in a bin. After performing this, your space should feel revitalised.

Enchanted Body and Skincare Items Spell

Combining this with the Mirror Work practice will aid in increasing your self-love. Self-love isn't just about appreciating your physical self and not being embarrassed by your body, but it is part of it! To perform this, gather the care items that you'd like to enchant. You can do this with one or many items, but if you want to narrow the choice down, it is most beneficial to choose the item which would go on the part of yourself that you have the least love and appreciation for.

At your sacred space, on a waxing Moon, light a candle (one 'dressed' to represent self-love, if you can), burn incense representative of self-love to you or similar to your power scent (see Fire chapter for more on this), and set the mood in any other way you feel appropriate.

Cast a circle if you'd like and take a few moments to calm and centre yourself. Sit comfortably and hold the objects to be enchanted in your hands. Close your eyes and breathe in the scents around you. Let them become a part of you and when you feel ready, focus into the feeling of love and the things that accompany it, like acceptance and unconditional positive regard.

See yourself in your mind's eye as you are sitting now and continue to feel that love. (If you struggle to visualise, modify this so you are sitting in front of a mirror so that you can see as much of yourself in it as possible).

Shift the focus of your gaze to the part of you that you want to love more and hold that feeling of love. If you notice a drop in your feeling, then place yourself for a moment in someone else's shoes whom you have known to admire that part of you before and feel the genuineness of that affection. Send it all of the love you are holding right now.

Zoom out again and focus on your whole Self. See yourself glowing with love and appreciation.

Holding onto that feeling, gently open your eyes and waft the smoke over the items you're holding and repeat the following:

'The love and appreciation I feel for myself now ebbs into this/these items. No matter how I may feel on any given day, I know that I can always step back into the presence of love and appreciation and gift myself with those feelings. Any time I use this/these items, I am showing myself love and appreciation, and my sense of this grows every time. So mote it be.'

You have now sealed in your intent for these items and may sit in this state for as long as you need to and then can close the circle/end the spell.

Healing doesn't mean the hurt never existed; it means it doesn't control your life anymore. – Akshay Dubey

Mirror Work – Appreciate Your Reflection

Self-love is evident in the way that you think of yourself, how you talk *to* and *about* yourself. You may be aware that some of your self-talk is very critical and disrespectful of your physical appearance. Change this now because this will be damaging your self-esteem and motivation and lowering your general vibration. If you aren't aware of what you say, and this goes for speaking about yourself and others, think of it like this: if the words you spoke appeared on your skin, would you still be beautiful?

To bring this home even more, record all the adjectives (descriptive words) you use about yourself for three days and see how many of them are positive versus negative, and you'll get an idea. As witches, we know that the words we use are super powerful. We speak into existence with what we say. Because of this, witchcraft is great for teaching you to *mind your language* and pay attention to your words, which essentially makes you kinder and more considerate to yourself and others.

As well as applying counter-statements (see page 112), tell yourself at least three things you are grateful for about your body and face as you look in the mirror, every day until you no longer need to (which may take a while). Challenge yourself to say different things throughout the week.

A particularly good time to do this is whilst body brushing or applying body lotion – all over your body, in front of a mirror (yes, for males too – everyone can take care of their bodies!) Take time to be loving and caring as you do so. You deserve it, and your body deserves it too.

Think of *everything* your body does for you and allows you to do – it deserves respect and compassion. If you're really stuck, pull out a biology book or video and marvel at all the intricate and complex processes that go on without much conscious awareness from you. That marvel alone can be a place to start.

Whatever you focus on grows, what you think about expands, and what you dwell upon determines your destiny. – Robin S. Sharma

Re-centre and Stabilise – Grounding Exercises

Grounding can be used whenever you feel a little off-kilter or 'spaced'. This usually happens when we have been too 'in our head', have experienced strong emotion, or strong energies during ritual or divination. You may also need to ground somewhat during certain transition times, such as before coming home from work, because otherwise you can be too rapidly 'switching' from one role to another and that can throw us off.

Experiment with the variations to find what works best for you, but essentially you become still, stabilise your breath, and imagine roots or a cord of light connecting from your feet right down into the centre of the Earth. Sometimes it's good to wrap the roots around a large chunk of a grounding stone such as black tourmaline.

Take some moments to send whatever feeling it is you don't want into the Earth to be neutralised and feel calmness flowing back into you via your feet. Of course, you can utilise physical crystals, such as smoky quartz, and stones that you find grounding and hold them until you feel calm during the visualisation.

You can also literally ground by putting your bare feet on grass or the floor and do the roots visualisation, which is sometimes known as 'Earthing'. Alternatively, because Earth is a supportive element, you may find great relief imagining yourself in a cave of your choosing or just sinking into a cocoon in the Earth.

If these things are a little too abstract for you, then you could try a mindful version of grounding which involves becoming aware of each of your five primary senses, paying particular attention to feeling your feet on the ground or your back against a chair, if applicable. This need only take a few moments, and you'll only look like you have drifted into a daydream if anyone notices you.

I personally find that drinking a grounding tea is helpful as well. Usually, this is made from vegetables of the Earth, such as beetroot and ginger. Anything is grounding so long as it feels as though it puts you back into your body and sense of Self, which means that stomping your feet, clapping your hands, sucking on a strong mint, naming objects seen, and playing with fidget-toys can be helpful.

Hearing a comforting and steady voice or receiving a hug are also ways to ground, especially if they're from someone you trust. This is when reaching out to people is good, even if it's just calling them up and asking them to talk to you for a bit. Nowadays, we can also create quick links back to favourite videos or episodes of podcasts if there's someone whose voice we find soothing to access if there's no one physically nearby or able to speak with. Or even have someone we love record a voice clip for us of them saying soothing things to us to play when they're not around.

Letting go doesn't mean forgetting, it just means we stop carrying the energy of the past into the present. – Yung Pueblo

Card Spread: Understanding and Breaking Bad Habits

This is a straight-forward spread designed to help you gain more clarity with any bad habits that you may feel that you have right now and to figure out how you can safely start to break out of the pattern of repeating them. I do not know who created this spread originally – it's been in my tarot journal for so long – but it is so useful because what we allow to be is what will continue to be.

1. Root cause of the habit – what's at the bottom of it.
2. Internal influences that exacerbate the habit for me.
3. External influences that aggravate the habit for me.
4. My strengths that I can use to break out of the habit.
5. An inspired action plan for the next three months.
6. A message of healing for comfort and motivation.

Earth Journal/Meditation Prompts and Action Points:

~What is happening in my external world at the moment?

~What does health mean to me?

~Really *why* do *I* want to live healthily?

~What motivates me to love and appreciate my body?

~What nutritional things do I need to learn more about?

~What helps *me* stay healthy?

~What key changes do I need to make to my lifestyle?

~What fitness blocks do I have that I need to alter?

~What changes do I need to make to my workout routine?

~What am I tired of that is holding me back?

~What can I consider reducing or eliminating in my life?

~What are my priorities for my health and wellness currently?

~What self-care practices do I need to start to gradually implement from now?

~My favourite places to escape to and make time for myself are …

~How should my outer world be if I am in alignment with my highest purpose, or at least *more* in alignment with it?

~What is it I actually need at present?

~What is one key short-term action, implementable immediately, to help me strengthen my connection to myself?

~What is the most empowering type of weather for me?

~Do the phases of the Moon influence me, and how?

~What's my favourite hour of the day and why?

~What's my favourite sight, sound, smell, and tactile experience that I've enjoyed recently?

~What aspects of my life can I celebrate/give thanks for?

~What aspects do I need to contemplate and change?

~What action points do I need to take to improve my current environment/surroundings? List these and diarise.

~What effective steps can I take in the coming weeks?

~List all of my favourite self-care activities and schedule them in throughout the upcoming months and weeks.

~Devise a list of alternative activities that I can do instead of something that I want to stop doing, and put it somewhere visible to prompt me when I go to do the thing I want to stop (creating an opportunity to choose differently and break my habit or destructive cycle).

~Create a wellness vision board. You can do this in sacred space by casting a circle and setting the ambience in any way you choose (music, scent, teas, etc.).

Arrange collections of images, words and sigils that represent the things that support your general sense of wellness on some thick card, poster board, or in a frame.

When you're happy with your arrangement, stick them down and as you do so, really feel as though you are solidifying these things into your life and feel the support that they give you.

You can keep this visible if you like to remind you of your dedication to your wellness and as a tool to remind you of what supports you have to your positivity, physical and mental health.

In any given moment we have two options: to step forward into growth or step back into safety. – Gabrielle Bernstein

Water

There is a stream
of love
supporting you

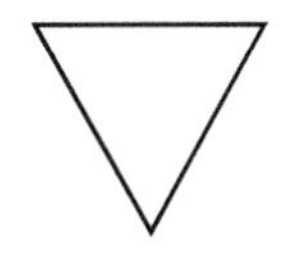

5: WATER ~ PART I
AS WITHOUT

I listen to my emotions but they do not rule me, I am connected with my intuition at all times – it serves me well.

***

Water is the realm of the social – our connections with others – and emotional wellness. It is the realm of the heart and love; emotions change just as Water is ever-transforming in its many forms. It's considered a slow/medium-paced element and is connected to theta brain waves which occur in flow states of consciousness. This chapter is looking at communication with others and making it healthy, productive, respectful, and effective. Your relationships evolve as you evolve. You become more skilled at navigating them and become a role model within them. The more you respect yourself, the more others show respect towards you, and they understand that crossing boundaries has consequences.

Connecting with Water

Water is such a cleansing and mysterious element. Most people have a strong opinion on Water. Where does your mind jump to when I ask what Water means to you?

As always, take a few moments to jot down your responses so that you may review them at a later date.

~What role does Water play in your daily life?

~Is it a necessity, a commodity or is it greatly looked forward to and appreciated?

~Do you have any strong memories connected to Water, and what do they mean to you now, and how do they influence you?

~Are there any natural places you enjoy to go to and connect with Water?

~Can you swim? If so, how does deep water make you feel, and if not, why have you not learnt?

~Do you like rain and storms – why or why not?

~How can you connect more to Water?

There are so many options with Water. Think about all the ways we can consume it (different types of tea and other hot/cold drinks) and cleanse with it. Washing, showering and bathing need not be elaborate rituals every time, but sometimes a decorated intention is a great indulgence!

Think of the different forms of water and how they enter into your life…ice, liquid, steam. It's versatile and adaptable, just how we are when we wear different hats throughout the day depending on what role we're in. The different versions of ourselves that we present to the world depending on where we are, who we're with, what we're doing, what our intentions are, and how we're feeling.

Just as Water can obscure, so can we present a less transparent version of ourselves to the world when we want to.

~Is that something you find yourself doing a lot?

~Which form of Water are you feeling most like currently?

~What's your boiling point/what tells you you've reached your limit?

~What's your freezing point/what's a value that is a no-no to cross with you?

~Are you riding the waves of life –' what helps you do that?

Wear your vulnerability like a crown; whether it's made of thorns or wildflowers is up to you. – Keerthana Nair

A Lesson from All of the Elements

Each element, in its own way, shows us the necessity and beauty of change and with that, the impermanence of everything. Sometimes that can be a truly scary thought, and we can become trapped in trying to *prevent* certain things from happening as a means to soothe the anguish, fear and dread of that thing coming to be, or control everything as a means to make a desired outcome certain, even though that just leads to anguish and pain and operating from fear again. We can try to rescue our future self from pain and heartache yet that will lead us to living very small lives. Recognise this as ego-based fear. As you're reading this, some things might be passing through your mind – perhaps it's death of a loved one, your own mortality, failure, heartache, embarrassment… ?

The most fertile soils are around volcanos. Plant life blooms and dies each year. Air helps trees shed dead leaves and branches so new ones can grow, it blows pollen seeds when other animals and insects do not carry them, and it allows clouds to travel. Water evaporates from oceans and lakes and makes its way back up into the mountains, drinkable again from source. Stars begin in stellar nurseries which are born from exploded stars that have completed their life cycle. Everything in nature is part of a cycle, and those were but a few rudimentary examples.

Change is a necessary part of life. You change physically as you grow and age, as you learn more things, as you have more experiences. It's okay to feel uncomfortable with change. Acknowledge that uncomfortable feelings often accompany change because growth isn't necessarily a comfortable process. Just as our skin can itch as it stretches to give us our adult skeleton and a pregnant woman's belly can itch as the baby grows, our spirit can kind of itch too. That's just what this is. Many of us can want to be out of the uncomfortable feeling as soon as possible and so rush what is happening or avoid it entirely. Notice what that is and reassure yourself that you may be uncomfortable, but you can handle it and know that the discomfort is temporary and leading you closer to what it is that you wanted from the change.

A Quick Connection Assessment Exercise for Clarity

It can help to get a visual on something because when we see diagrams, they often help make something abstract easier to comprehend and view more objectively. For this, take a piece of scrap paper or your journal and write 'Me' in the centre of it and draw a circle around it.

Think of the people with whom you spend the *most* time and write their name on the page, putting a circle around them too – bigger if it's a lot of time and smaller if not so much. Repeat this until you have included all of the people you are most frequently in the company of.

Take a different coloured pen and write a number next to each person's name based upon the nature of their impact on you on a scale of 0-10, or 0-100 if that would be more appropriate for you. Zero means completely negative – you hate being around them and always leave their company feeling totally awful in some way; and the maximum means that you feel amazing around them, really happy and contented.

Who is having the biggest impact on you, and what can be done to improve the connection? Is there anything else you're dissatisfied with and what can you change to have it be more desirable? Is there anyone you need to shorten time spent with or increase time spent with?

You should be left with a useful visual representation of what's going on for you in terms of connections with others and have some action points of changes to make.

Maintaining Healthy Relationships - Boundaries

Just because people are close to you or you live with them doesn't give them a free pass to treat you however they please. This is especially common within families and households. When one person is stressed or had a rough day, they can have a tendency to take it out on those around them, snap at them or be mean, simply because it feels safer to do so with those people, because love is unconditional – right? Nope. Love does not mean you need to accept how other people treat you – you can influence how others treat you. Likewise, become mindful of how you are acting towards others. Are you caught in a cycle with anyone in particular?

Getting clear on your own boundaries, communicating them to others and enforcing them is one of the most self-loving things you can do. You are showing people how you want to be treated and that you respect yourself; in time, they will have no choice but to follow suit or be left in your wake. If you are struggling to understand boundaries that you may have, you may find it useful to assess your values, which is covered in the Fire chapter. The most effective way to communicate boundaries with others is through assertive communication …

No one can make you feel inferior without your consent.
– Eleanor Roosevelt

Hold onto Your Power Respectfully – Assertiveness

Assertiveness is a way of communicating that is respectful to yourself, your needs and rights, and the other person in the interaction and their needs and rights. It's helpful to understand it as a productive form of communication, as opposed to passive or aggressive forms. A sign that communication skills can be improved is if you frequently have conversations with different people and feel unheard. This is frustrating and can lead to resentment and other hurts. Communication happens in every area of life, and sometimes, a healthy conversation will end with agreeing to disagree – and that's okay. Through practice, assertive communication will become natural; patience is definitely required with this one, but once it clicks, it has great benefits and can make many things a lot simpler!

It's worth noting that you may already communicate assertively in some situations, but not realise that you use a different form with other people or in some situations. Passive communication looks like putting the needs of others totally at the detriment of your own, which serves to undermine your sense of self-worth, and usually leaves you feeling relatively unhappy. The body language of someone being passive is usually small – they almost shrink themselves and tend to 'take up' less space. They typically speak quietly, slowly, and avoid the gaze of the person they're talking with, and may fidget. What is said may be quite submissive, unsure, self-deprecating, vague, or overly apologetic and reserved.

Aggressive communication, on the other hand, is neglecting others over yourself and can often leave you and the other person feeling bad about the interaction with you. It generally involves being loud, quick, over-using eye-contact (glaring), dramatic gesticulating, anger, and can involve heavy sarcasm, swearing, demanding, shaming, interrupting, patronising, mocking, criticising unconstructively, blaming, insulting, controlling, and arguing.

Assertiveness is the healthy balance between these two extremes and aims to leave all conversation participants feeling the interaction was fair and that they were all heard. It's not a license to say anything you want; you still need to be polite, reasonable and tactful with what you say.

It is a confident form of speaking calmly, clearly and concisely (without ambiguity) and listening to the other person, and is also translated into polite and relaxed body language, as no one is getting defensive, upset or frustrated. The tone of voice with assertiveness is respectful but firm; the pace is steady, and eye-contact feels easy and appropriate.

One of the keys of assertive conversation is using what are called 'I statements', such as 'I feel …' or 'I would like …' which are particularly useful when something needs to be resolved as they feel less accusatory and softer to the other person than when you start the sentence with 'you': 'you didn't …'.

I statements make use of your thoughts and feelings to help the conversation remain on a human-to-human level that, under normal circumstances, sets up the participants for sympathy or empathy which improves the chances of the conversation being calm and respectful, e.g. 'I feel worried when you don't let me know you'll be coming home late.' Using the right emotion in a sentence informs the listener why what you're saying is important and puts it into perspective, for example, 'I've been feeling frustrated about doing much of the house chores. I understand you're busy, but I need some more help, please. How can we make this work?'

If assertive communication is unusual to you and you would like to practice it to build your confidence with it first, a good way is to consider some past interactions you have had and reflect on how you would have responded or started the conversation if you were assertive. You could also take inspiration from fictional characters, like those in books and on screen.

The more you wrap your head around how assertive communication looks, sounds, and feels, the easier it will be for you to carry it through in your real life. You may like to rehearse with someone trusted, and when you feel ready, it helps to pick one thing or situation to be assertive with to start. Be clear with your needs and wishes and rehearse what you'll say. This could be something simple, such as asking for tea instead of coffee if someone frequently assumes that is what you want.

It isn't always possible to make all parties happy all of the time; compromise is a necessary part of life. However, you can still have respectful discussions to reach a compromise, and sometimes, you will need to say no clearly and search for a different solution.

Be who you are and say what you feel because those who mind don't matter and those who matter don't mind. – Dr. Seuss

The Power of Acting True to Yourself - Saying No

You may identify that you have a tendency to people-please. Perhaps you fear disappointing others or struggle with the thought that they may dislike you if you disagree with them. Note that this is a self-esteem issue on your part and your ego is in the driver's seat with this one. It's not an easy habit to kick, but that's exactly it. You have gotten used to saying yes because it feels easier, less conflicting. Once you commit to acting in alignment with your greatest good, changing your behaviour in this area becomes easier. If it does not serve you to say yes to something, then pause and politely decline.

Here is a perfect time to practice assertiveness and the I statements described above. Note that you may feel uncomfortable with this initially, but it is because it is unusual for you, both to do and to hear no from yourself. You may also be unaccustomed to the reaction you see from others at your saying no. They simply are reacting to novelty too. You will both become used to it the more it occurs, and eventually, it will be natural for you to assess whether it is best for you to say yes or no in a situation.

Saying no isn't about being unhelpful, not compromising (being in-flexible), or passing over opportunities that could be good for you, even though the thought of the opportunity is a little scary because it's outside your comfort zone. It is about understanding yourself fully and acting in alignment with what best serves you and others. If someone is genuinely asking for your help and you actually have the time and energy and want to assist – that's great – say yes! If saying yes would actually cause you problems and force you to pour from an empty cup, then sensitively say no.

The delivery of the no is what allows you to still maintain a strong and healthy connection with the other person. Do so assertively and sensitively and if you want to enter into a compromise, offer what you are willing and able to do as an alternative and go from there. Saying no to the wrong things for you allows the right things to come into your life that your whole self wants to say yes to!

Devaluing a 'Sorry' – Over-apologising

Develop the habit of only apologising when you truly mean it. Not only will you feel better for this but others who truly love and value you will respect you for it as well. Sometimes we apologise to 'keep the peace' and because it seems like 'the right thing to do'. Ultimately though, over-apologising is a sure-fire way to take power from yourself and cheapen the value of a true apology when it is earnestly meant.

If you struggle to apologise when you actually are sorry, it's likely to be a pride issue that you are having. Pride shows up as a defensive manoeuvre when we are tying in our sense of self-worth to whatever it is that we are sorry for. To apologise is to admit fault, and those of us with perfectionist streaks can especially struggle with this. Learn to separate your sense of self-worth from always being and doing right and see the situation from the other person's perspective. If you would like them to apologise to you, chances are this is what you ought to do in this situation as well. Swallow the pride and search for the sincere part of you that holds compassion and apologise from that part of you – from the heart.

If need be, silently ask your guides, the Universe, etc., for strength in the moment to do what is right. It gets easier with time the more often you do this.

Relationship Quality over Quantity

If you are feeling misunderstood by those around you or that your interactions with others are unsatisfactory – you don't feel great after being in a conversation with someone else – then it may be that the quality of that relationship is a little off, especially if this is the case after boundaries have been communicated and implemented.

Consider whether the time spent communicating with this person needs to be limited so that the quality can be there. This doesn't have to be a drastic change in how much you see or speak to them. You can gradually decrease the time until it reaches that point where you leave an interaction with them feeling simply good and that it was worthwhile.

To assist with considering the quality of a relationship, you can ask yourself these questions and journal your answers for later reflection:

~How often do you and this person talk uninterrupted, without distraction, in a week (or month if more appropriate)?

~Do you evade particular topics in order to avoid conflict?

~When you feel this person has been unfair to you or judgmental, how do you usually react?

~How quickly do you resolve disagreements and move forwards again?

~Do you have apologies accepted by this person respectfully or are you expected to practically grovel?

~Do they ever *sincerely* apologise to you and then enact the appropriate behaviour changes?

~Do you ever feel empty, hollow or bad after interacting with this individual/group?

~Do you feel listened to and understood by this person?

Depending on your answers to these questions, you may need to examine whether this is actually something that can be improved or if it is a toxic connection for you. If you decide that it is toxic, then please read the next exercise below.

Relationship Clarity Exercise

Humans are social animals, and it is beneficial for our wellbeing to connect with others, even for the most introverted of people. However, sometimes, despite communicating assertively, implementing boundaries, saying no and trying to improve the quality of the connection, some relationships just don't feel good. Yet even though you may be coming to the conclusion that maybe it isn't such a great idea to keep this person in your life, it can be difficult to let them go. Maintaining a relationship that has run its course or even a toxic connection is really emotionally demanding, if not also stressful and time-consuming.

The more you build your self-love and value yourself, the harder it is to keep such a connection because you can no longer tolerate the harm or pain that it causes you. We can strengthen the part of you that recognises this connection needs to go by gathering evidence that it is the best course of action. You can answer the following questions for each person you have a connection with that feels a bit 'off', not as great as it once was, unhealthy, or is questionable:

~What was the purpose of this connection initially?

~Has that purpose been met and is it still necessary now?

~Is there another form this connection can take that is less intense for me/demanding of my personal resources?

~Why was this connection so important to me?

~Why is this connection so harmful/negative for me?

~How has this connection impacted things in my past?

~How does this relationship affect other things in my present life, including how I behave and feel?

~Have I tried everything reasonable and realistic to improve the connection whilst still respecting myself?

~Am I wanting this person to be something they aren't?

~Is this person able to meet my realistic expectations?

~What is their responsibility and not in my control?

~Is there anything I can take responsibility for between us that may improve the connection if I want it to be stronger?

~Is this connection really that important to me now?

~Are our values complementary or always in opposition?

You may then conclude that the connection cannot continue for your own wellbeing or that it has run its course. You can then choose to communicate this to the other person if it is safe to do so, or ask another person or an organisation to support you or provide further advice in terminating this relationship safely.

If you want to know what a man's really like, look at how he treats his inferiors, not his equals. – Sirius Black (Harry Potter)

Empower Yourself – Expand Emotional Vocabulary

When we have the most accurate word for what we're feeling, we allow ourselves and others to more precisely respond to our feelings. To help with this, it can be useful to photograph or print out an *emotion wheel* (type it into your image search engine; I prefer the one created by the Junto Institute). Oftentimes we may identify one of the primary emotions at the centre of the wheel, such as sadness, when in fact, what we are experiencing is more complex or nuanced and more like say, feeling hurt. Usually, we experience one of the emotions on the outer wheel and it evolves into one in the centre because it is ignored. Once we have the exact words for what we're experiencing, it's also more likely that we can move forwards from them because we can better see where they have come from, how to prevent them occurring again from this situation if they're undesirable, self-soothe, and move on.

The Way Out is Through – Processing Emotions

Emotions are information: they carry a message, and it is up to us to take the time, be it a few moments or longer, to interpret the message of that information, and then act upon it or not. Sometimes though, it feels as though the emotion is lingering, and consciously acknowledging its message isn't enough. This is particularly the case with the lower end of the emotional spectrum – the emotions we often tend to label as negative and unhelpful, such as frustration or sadness.

Many readers will find that they can meditate or practice some mindfulness or breathing techniques, and that is enough to help them process through an emotion and let it go to invite in something else that they want. Other times that isn't quite as effective or simply doesn't work. You may need to go through some 'trial and error' work here. Reflect and list what has helped you work through emotions in the past.

Next, write down any other techniques or tools that you think could be helpful for you; you can include things you have heard that friends and family do that work for them.

Once you've done that, cross off anything you may have written that you *do not* want to do. This could be something that you recognise is actually a pretty destructive or harmful practice. You should be left with a good few options now. You may write these out neater on a clean piece of paper, and you now have a set of healthy techniques, activities and mechanisms that you can use next time you need one to help you with an emotion that you feel a bit stuck with.

To help you out if you have only a few ideas, the following are particularly helpful.

Put on some songs that you really enjoy singing and can do with pure abandon (I do this while driving sometimes if I want a good sing but know there's going to be people at home – I'm a private singer!) Singing causes a re-set of breath as you have to breathe into your diaphragm, which leads to more oxygen reaching your brain, thereby improving mental alertness and memory. It also increases stamina and is akin to a cardio workout if you really project your voice; it releases endorphins, decreases blood levels of cortisol, and so de-stresses you, and has shown to increase antibodies in some people, thereby strengthening their immune system. Many people report the cathartic benefits of singing, and you don't actually need to be a 'good' singer to benefit from it. It's one of the fastest-acting mood changers, so bite the bullet and give it a go.

Another way is to move. Movement can be in the form of a brisk walk, yes, but the key to help process emotion, to allow expression to play a part; and while a fresh-air walk can certainly calm you down sometimes and give you a change of scenery, it doesn't quite hit the spot that dancing can (if it does for you, then carry on with it, by all means!)

Emotions can be processed with any form of dance. The easiest and most accessible version for most people is putting on some favourite songs that you can't help but feel the rhythm with and letting your body flow with the music. Having space to do your best 'wacky-waving-inflatable-arm-flailing-tube-man' impression is great but totally not necessary. Dancing has very similar benefits to singing and is an easy and fun way to get aerobic exercise in, since you can dance to what you like and how you please. Dancing with another person has been shown to particularly help decrease stress tension and joining a class has all the benefits of socialising in a positive group. Dance takes your mind off thoughts as you have to concentrate in a different way to coordinate your body and maintain balance.

Movement is also a means to unlock stored emotional trauma in the limbic system (activated during trauma through the sympathetic nervous system or 'fight, flight, freeze' response when the prefrontal cortex goes 'offline') and work to coordinate parts of the brain that have become 'disconnected' and move the emotion to the rational brain (neocortex) where it can be cognitively reasoned with. There are specialist groups that therapeutically take you through a form of movement therapy (such as trauma-focused yoga) to gently help you process through what may come up.

The third powerful example I can give is expressive art, which is simply you taking any blank slate (digital art works too) and running wild with it. Use colours, form, texture – anything. Just *do*. You don't need to think. It's not the higher processing part of your brain that's engaged when planning what to do next as you're creating something. It's creating for the sake of creating – for the action of it.

A helpful alternative to creation with abandon can be to create a personification of your emotion – and it doesn't need to be a human; it can be a creature or anything else.

WATER ~ PART II
SO WITHIN

Water your roots so that your soul can blossom. – Unknown

***

Understand Your Feelings More Specifically – Mood Track

The emotion wheel (see page 89) can also be used to help you monitor the different emotions you feel throughout the day; there are also apps that can help with noting them. A good time to do this would be when you feel as though you always feel a particular emotion, such as anger, sadness, anxiousness or apathy.

Decide how frequently you will note your mood, whether hourly, more, or less. Then set alarms on your phone or watch to remind you to note the emotions you have experienced in the set time period. Get specific. You will most likely realise that you do experience different feelings, and this is great for your mental health. Even if the feelings aren't the type of emotions you'd wish to experience, at least the story is more complex than you have believed.

The next step would be to reflect on what is leading to the emotions you feel and assess whether you want more or less of them and how (consider the ways of cultivating and minimising emotions in this book!)

Don't hide in the shadows because someone can't handle your light.
– Ara Campbell

Be Gently Steered to Feel Different - Guided Meditation

With these, you are in a state of surrender as you focus only on the words you hear and follow the instructions. You can choose different guided meditations that work for you and save them to a playlist or folder for whenever you need. They can be a great way to begin your day by empowering you, or end your day by releasing any stress or worries so you can sleep.

Guided meditations are particularly helpful if you feel you are not ready to sit in silence or with music as your mind is too busy. Because you focus fully on the voice and follow the instructions, you are more likely to feel a benefit afterwards, as opposed to stressing that you can't clear your thoughts or let them pass without attending to them.

This form of meditation can also be used as a method of witnessing more of your unconscious mind as you are steered to think of different things and later reflect upon what you experienced. Anything that allows you to tap into your unconscious ultimately builds self-awareness.

The more you are in love with your life, the less you need others to be.

A Self-love Letter

This is a particularly good exercise to do whenever you feel really let down or hurt, and your self-esteem has taken a knock. Writing letters to your future-self and marking the envelope with a date to open it in the future can be a really powerful experience.

You can write to yourself now, in the present and/or write to yourself in the future. There are also ways of scheduling emails to yourself for future dates, if you wanted to type instead of write a physical letter.

If you are someone who associates handwritten letters with care and attention though, you may like to continue on physical paper as you already have an association that mirrors the intent of this activity.

Set up your sacred space so that it is a nurturing environment for this task and prepare to let yourself express yourself in the letter.

Have rose quartz crystals around you as these hold a very gentle and loving vibe for many and can support you with this task.

Address the letter to yourself and keep your writing positive. Steer away from insecurities and focus on the facts of what you love and like about yourself. Write about the things that make you unique and what you're proud of. You can start with 'Dear [your name], I love …' and write what you love about yourself.

You can also invoke a child-like sense of yourself if you'd like, from a time when you were completely happy with who you were. If you're struggling, place yourself in your friend's or family's shoes to see what they love about you and what they're grateful for about you.

If you write this for the present, add it to your self-love/wellness toolbox and read it whenever you need a boost to remind you that you are worthy, loveable, and capable – because you are.

Psychic Protection – Light Bubble Shield

Whether you're an energetically sensitive person or not, you may wish to add another layer of energetic protection to yourself. If you can't help being around negative people (such as at work or school) or you're simply going to a crowded place and want help to not have your energy influenced so much by others, then this can be very helpful.

Preferably before you leave your home, enter into a quiet state of mind and close your eyes. Centre your attention on your heart chakra (located by your heart/or wherever feels right for you) and imagine a light glowing there.

The colour of this light is up to you. As you breathe in, imagine gathering your personal power and energy. And as you breathe out, see the light starting to expand, similar to a balloon or bubble. With each breath out, this light expands until it fully encircles your entire body.

Take a few moments to feel peaceful and safe within this bubble. Then set the intention of this shield – what types of energies will it let in, if any, and what will it keep out? Inside the bubble is all the love and peace that you need.

I like to imagine the light of mine as forming a type of intelligent mesh which lets in only the energy I allow, such as the love of others, and also allows me to project the energies I want out too, such as my love and happiness.

Throughout the day, you can see your bubble in your mind's eye and draw comfort in the knowledge that it is there to help you. I also sometimes imagine directly projecting an emotion through my bubble to another person, such as the comfort of compassion if I see they need support in a moment.

Equally, if you are struggling in a moment, you can imagine light from the Cosmos drawing to your bubble to strengthen it, and see the negativity or harmful energies from others being deflected and falling to the Earth to be neutralised.

Allow this bubble to help you lovingly and joyfully claim your space and shine your light within the world, without compromising your integrity, and help others by encouraging them to do the same.

Worry about loving yourself instead of how much others love you.

Cleansing Ritual Bath

This can be adapted if you do not have a bath and if a shower isn't enough for you alone; it can work well by substituting the bathing part for a bowl that's deep and wide enough to soak your feet in.

For this ritual you may like to consider which of the following components you can choose that represent cleansing to you: a candle, an incense/herb bundle, an oil (safe for the skin in water), crystal (that's ok to go in water or get wet, *note* Selenite is not water-safe), and Epsom salt.

To begin, I always prefer to take a shower first so that I actually feel clean and fresh, ready for the ritual part to commence. I use the time to stabilise my thoughts and settle them on my intention for the ritual, then rinse the bathtub and run the water.

While the tub's filling, cleanse the room with the incense/herb bundle and light the candle (dress it first if you want to, see page 27 for how). Pour in the Epsom salt and several drops of your oil and enter the water.

When the tub's filled to your liking, turn off the taps, hold your crystal to your chest and lie back.

Meditate on cleansing yourself of any unwanted and unhelpful energies to your highest good, for as long as you like with the aid of the water, because we are letting go to create space for something better.

When you feel as though you have released them, turn your intentions towards what energies you would like to replace them with. What is it you'd like to feel more of at the moment?

If you work with any form of archetype, guide, deity or being, now would be a good time to ask for their assistance with helping you bring more of the energy you desire into your life.

Naturally, this ritual lends itself to specific beings that are aligned with water, so they can be particularly useful to connect with at this time. Take your time settling into the emotions of your intention.

Once you feel as though you are filled up with the energy, rise and empty the bath. Visualise your unwanted energies going down the drain and being neutralised by the Earth and know they are no longer yours.

Turn your attention to patting yourself dry and moisturising to 'seal in' the desired energy while saying 'With this lotion, I seal in my intent to feel … and so it is.'

If you are to love, love as the moon loves; it does not steal the night – it only unveils the beauty of the dark. – Isra Al-Thibeh

Negativity Banishing Spell

Sometimes there may be someone who you don't want to cut out of your life, yet they still carry a lot of negativity around with them; perhaps they are judgemental and generally bring the vibe down a notch or two. Respect yourself and your space with this spell to make it so that person cannot spread negativity into your space. You may like to perform this spell on a waning Moon (to diminish their negativity in your space) and repeat it annually if you feel it necessary.

You will need: a pestle and mortar; a cauldron (or fire-proof bowl); a tea-light in a colour that represents protection for you (I choose black); a photo of the person (or a personal effect of theirs such as some hair from their brush if you don't have a photo); a piece of paper and pen in corresponding colours; any dried plants that represent protection and negativity-banishment, such as rosemary, rowan leaves, blackberry leaves; and some salt or black salt if you have that.

You can also place some protective crystals around your working area or altar while you do this spell, such as smoky quartz, onyx, mahogany obsidian, jet, black tourmaline, howlite, red tiger's eye, or even petrified wood.

Cast a circle, except this time, extend it out over your whole property, because the spell is to affect the whole of your space. When you are calm and centred, take the paper and create a sigil (see page 165 for sigil creation) that focuses on protecting your space from this person's negativity. Because this is a sigil relating to another person, you may include their name or initials in some way if that feels right to you.

Once you're happy with your sigil, draw that into the candle if you can; don't worry if it's too complex or large for the candle, though. Take the mortar and pestle and grind together the herbs you've selected, with intent. Imagine that as they are ground, they are releasing their magickal properties of negativity-banishment and protection from negativity and becoming more potent.

In the cauldron, place the photo of the person and sprinkle the ground herbs on top.

If you have a banishing or protection oil, you can dress the candle with that in a bottom-to-wick motion, or simply use a corresponding oil of a herb you've used.

Light the candle and place it in the cauldron.

As it burns chant with conviction the following nine times (the power of three by three by three and magickal completion): *'(Full name of the person), I bind you from speaking ill in my space. If you intend to be negative in my home, you will promptly feel like leaving. You are not allowed to be critical and mean in my place.'*

As the candle burns, see the person standing at your door and the negative words they have drying up in their mouth and falling away to the Earth to be neutralised. See that as they enter your space, they pass through your energetic filter, and they are not able to be negative here.

Leave the candle to safely burn itself out. When the wax and any embers have cooled, gather the contents of the cauldron into a black pouch or painted glass jar and paint on to it the sigil. Close the circle and place this somewhere safe and unseen.

If you like, you can always paint the sigil on the underside of a doormat or draw it with chalk or oil under a mat as a further negativity trap before this person visits.

You can't stop the waves but you can learn to surf. – Jon K. Zinn

Poppet Self-love and Healing Spell

Poppets are useful little creations for many types of spellwork as they represent a form of sympathetic magick, which is having a physical representation of the thing one wishes to have influence over. This spell utilises a poppet, which is a simple miniature 'doll', usually made of cloth, to represent yourself, and is especially suitable when you are consciously working on healing through something emotional and you want to surround yourself with as much love as possible to aid in the healing that you're doing – because love is especially good at healing emotional wounds, although it helps with mental and physical ones too!

For this, you will need: some fabric (preferably in a colour that represents you); a needle and thread or fabric glue; a couple of strands of your hair; and anything to stuff the poppet with, such as wadding, cotton wool and/or dried flowers (like rose petals), crystal chips of rose quartz, and a tiny scroll of paper, etc.

This spell can take a while so it may be a good idea to have a drink on hand, such as the Sensuali-tea (see page 63).

Cast a circle if you'd like and perform during the waxing Moon.

Cut two simple 'gingerbread person' shapes with a two-centimetre seam allowance from your material. The poppet only need be as tall as your hand.

Depending on your material, you may find it best to sew or glue the fabric, right sides together and leaving a gap at the top of its head so you can fill it.

Once you have left enough room for a gap in the top (about big enough for you to get two thumbs inside), carefully turn it inside out.

Gather the fillings for your little poppet version of you, including the hair, and as you carefully fill it (you can use the end of a chopstick, wand, or pencil to push the filling so it fills nicely into the arms and legs, if necessary), imagine that you are calling to yourself all of the loving, positive, healing, and hopeful energies that you need to support you at this time.

Repeat a mantra out loud if you like while you fill and visualise these energies creating a loving glow around you, such as, 'I let go of emotional wounds that no longer serve me. I give and receive love freely. I am love and love is all around me.'

On the little scroll write 'I heal through love, and I have all the love that I need and more' or choose your own words, and pop the scroll into the poppet.

Place your poppet somewhere safe on your altar, perhaps on a bed of rose petals and, if you have them, surround it with rose quartz or jade and other crystals and objects that represent love and healing to you.

Every day, take time to sit with your poppet; meditate, visualise, and feel the love surrounding you. Light a scented candle blessed for healing and love while you do this as well to make it even more potent (see page 27 for how).

Do this until you have completed your healing for a full Moon cycle or until the Moon is full, whichever is first/feels best to you.

Store your poppet safely away when you're not actively using it, because it can be used again to represent you in future spell work.

The wound is the place where the light enters you. – Rumi

Card Spread: Deep Self-Love, by Kelly-Ann Maddox

This spread is designed to help you with the daily practice of self-love and understand what would support you best with that at this current time.

1. How to honour who you were in the past whilst embracing who you are now.

2. Acknowledging your efforts, strengths and abilities.

3. Developing more personal power and wielding it effectively.

4. Recognising the voice of the inner critic/bully and dealing with it.

5. How your life could improve with a daily self-love practice.

6. Suggested regular self-love practices.

7. How to keep going when dealing with self-doubt/self-loathing.

When you make a conscious choice to be happy, no-one can take it away from you because no-one gave it to you: you gave it to yourself.
– Emma Mumford

Water Journal/Meditation Prompts and Action Points:

~What is taking up space in my heart right now?

~What feels uncomfortable about my life right now?

~What is happiness for me – and what does it look like?

~What is helping to make me feel happy currently?

~How will happiness impact me and the people in my life?

~What brings me/gives me emotional strength?

~Who makes me laugh?

~Who do I definitely enjoy being around?

~Is there anyone I haven't listed as enjoying being around who I do spend time with regularly?

~What does friendship mean to me?

~What do I value most in a friendship?

~How can I be generous to myself?

~How can I be generous to others within my means?

~What role does affection play in my life, and what does it mean for me?

~List five things that I like about my physical self.

~List five things that I like about my non-physical self.

~What is my favourite quality or trait about myself?

~How can I recognise the beauty within others?

~What key strengths and abilities do I possess that help within relationships? (Not just romantic, but any type.)

~How can I best handle other people's emotions?

~What is a personal boundary I need to implement straight away?

~What patterns do I keep repeating in my relationships?

~What issue from my past is still influencing me currently?

~Where am I wearing a mask or deceiving myself at all?

~What attachments from my past need to be addressed that are hindering my growth/joy (not just with people)?

~How can I find a sense of closure or relief from a painful attachment or situation ending?

~What connections do I want to strengthen and improve?

~What do I need to let go of in order to emotionally heal?

~Where/in what contexts do I display courage?

~How can I nurture myself at this time?

~What role does love play in my life?

~What fears are holding me back?

~Which of these fears are ego-fears and therefore limiting?

~Which of these fears, if any, are phobias?

~What actions can I take to support myself in facing, challenging, and overcoming these fears?

~What is one key short-term action, implementable immediately, to help me strengthen my connection to love?

~What are the main five emotions I want to feel daily?

~Who do I take advice from, and why do I heed them?

~Do I need to expand my circle of advisors or supporters?

~List all of the sources of support I have and what exactly they support me with. (Add this to my self-care toolbox.)

~What expressive activities can I do that allow my mind to 'switch off' in a good way and just engage mindfully with the present moment? (These are often things that occupy our hands, i.e. arts and crafts, mindfulness colouring books, cooking, photography, woodworking, creative makeup and hair play, up-cycling projects, DIY, etc.)

I see your darkness and raise you my light. - *Cassie Uhl*

Air

What you think
is what you
create

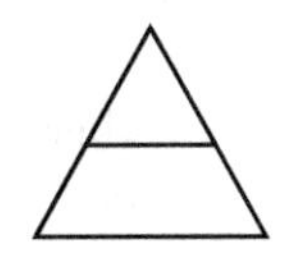

6: AIR ~ PART I
AS ABOVE

My mind is a place of peace and clarity. I have creative and brilliant ideas often and I choose my thoughts wisely with intention.

***

Air is the mind, thoughts and imagination. It's considered a medium-paced element and is coupled to alpha brain waves, which occur when relaxed yet awake – ideally when learning and interested. This section aims to assist you in creating your mind to be your best friend, a mind of positivity, rational thoughts, and realistic optimism that is helpful to you and by extension to others. You will get clear on what is going on in your mind, your internal dialogue, beliefs about yourself, others, and the world, and learn techniques to assist with undesired emotional states so that you can *feel, think, and respond* rather than feel only and react.

Connecting to Air

Have a ponder about what the Air element means to you. Take fifteen or so minutes to journal so you can record your thoughts. Do you have any significant memories that strongly involve Air? How does those memories influence what that element means to you, and the role it currently plays in your life? How would you describe Air if it was personified? Perhaps get creative and draw/paint/collage this Air archetype. Are you someone who spends a lot of time in their mind? Do you enjoy planning and researching?

Do you enjoy being in your own company – why/why not? Are you attracted to 'airy' colours or do you find yourself wearing them often? Are you slightly more contented in larger spaces or rooms with higher ceilings? How are you with large open spaces and high places – do you feel invigorated in them, small, or something else? How do you connect to Air in your life? How would you like to deepen your understanding and connection with this element? What jumps out to you as a way it can support you with your wellness moving forwards? Would you say you're more often logical than emotional?

An easy way to connect to Air is to become mindful of your posture – sit up straight and allow your lungs to be able to expand without restriction. Breathe. Feel the air at your nostrils and as it moves through you and back out again. You need it to live – are you acknowledging it? If no, then there's one thing right there to start! How about fresh air? Do you get outside often enough? Do you throw open your windows every now and again and let new air in to refresh your space? What scents are carried on the air – outside and in? Go outside when it's windy and feel the air brushing away stale energy, leaving you invigorated.

Asking for Support Wherever You Are - Prayer

If you hold certain beliefs about divinity, the Cosmos, spirit guides or ancestors, etc., you may find using prayer helpful to empower you over the unwanted thoughts. As soon as you notice the thought, tell it *no*, recognise it was your ego's misguided attempt to help you, and say a prayer for help that feels right to you; trust you'll be helped and then let it go. You may receive guidance or simply feel relief. Some ideas are: *'I surrender that thought to be transmuted by the Universe, thank you.' 'Thank you, Spirit, for guiding me to perceive this fear through the teacher of love.' 'I choose my thoughts; please help me, Guides to choose loving thoughts, thank you.' 'Please assist me, Cosmos, to reconnect to my joyful thoughts, thank you.' 'Please show me what I need to feel free of this emotion, and let it be for my highest good and the good of all.'*

Breaking Resistance to Asking for Support or Help

Psychotherapy is very useful for many people struggling with mental wellness. Perhaps your emotions feel too entrenched or tangled up with other things going on in your life, or you simply want to speak with someone about what is going on/has gone on who's not involved.

Finding a therapist that you connect well with and can trust to guide you can be a wonderful way of working through any problems to get you to a better version of yourself and your life. It can be a place of stability and consistency when your life feels far from that, and it can be a safe space to vent, develop self-awareness and work on your blocks to growth.

I've had counselling at a few points in my life now to help me along and give me that extra support during difficult times, so I understand how invaluable it can be from both sides of the coin. There are lots of ways to work with professionals to help you through blocks or stagnant emotions and process trauma safely, such as reiki, trauma-focused hypnotherapy, or EMDR (eye-movement desensitisation and reprocessing therapy).

There was a time when I believed that asking for help meant that I was weak (read: less valuable as a human), and felt shame at the thought or guilt for 'burdening' myself on someone else (all too commonly said by my clients too), but this wasn't my true belief: it was what other people had impressed upon me. I wanted to ask for help, even with the small things – that *is* self-love and care.

So, start with the 'small' things, like help understanding that computer programme, cooking, understanding an assignment, or sorting your finances. The more comfortable you get asking for help with the little things and before something becomes a problem, the easier it is for you to feel able to ask for help with the bigger or more emotional issues.

Anxiety does not empty tomorrow of its sorrows, but only today of its strength. – Charles Spurgeon

Bring Awareness – Thought Log

A lot of thoughts that we have tend to be more in the background of our mind, more in the subconscious rather than our forefront thoughts that happen in working memory, or our 'thinking mind'. If we are not careful, these background thoughts can become unproductive, negative, judgmental and harmful to our self-esteem. At worst, the mind can go into a type of black hole as the thoughts suck you in and get the better of you.

What begins as one intrusive thought can become an overwhelming concept if it's continually indulged with negative thinking. Sometimes you may find yourself filling silence with noise, any noise, just so you don't hear your own thoughts. I definitely had this for a time, and after doing the practices that follow, I was soon able to look forward to time when I could be alone with my thoughts.

The way to start to change the mind to be a productive place is first to become aware of what is happening there – what the landscape of your mind actually looks like. Then you can start pulling up the weeds, one by one.

Every time you notice a thought that is unhelpful, unkind, a judgment, negative comparison for yourself to someone else, or a disempowering story – note it down. Just capture it in a notebook or jot it onto a note in your phone if you don't have a notebook with you.

Get used to noticing this type of 'thought-weed' and capturing it, just as an observer does in a research study – witness it and note it down.

Once you capture a thought, if you can, complete the following or write the thought down and come back to this at the end of the day or as soon as you are able; then divide a page with the following columns:

Thought | Event | Emotions | Sensations | Behaviours

An example may be:

T: 'She ignored me at lunch; she must hate me.'

E: Sitting eating lunch when Xena walked straight by me.

E: Felt sad, anxious, confused, a little disappointed.

S: Chest felt a bit tight and a mild tummy ache.

B: Obsessing over what I have said or done to her lately, which made it difficult to concentrate; didn't enjoy my food; felt uncomfortable in the office later. Felt worried in case I have upset her – don't want her to dislike me.

This allows you to understand what is happening in your mind, the automatic thoughts you have and the effects of them. If the effects are negative or unproductive it shows that you need to alter what is happening in your mind – you need to pull out the weeds and dried leaves cluttering it up, and plant seeds for new beautiful flowers to thrive.

Cognitive psychology teaches that we have different types of automatic thoughts, and when they link to distress, they are often negative. These warp our perspective and thus our experience. Our thoughts create our reality and so what you think is what you feel. Like attracts like. The more you have negative thoughts and feelings about yourself, the more you will have negative experiences, because you will be eroding your self-esteem and feeling bad, and so responding to others and situations as someone who does not like, care for, or believe in themselves does. Which means you will have more unhelpful thoughts which gives poor experiences and so the cycle continues.

If this continues for long enough, we form beliefs around these feelings, and we now have a negative focus, so no matter what happens, we struggle to see a situation for its truth or at least from other perspectives without jumping to conclusions first. We can develop a type of mesh grid around us that only lets through one type of shape rather than all of the possible shapes, and so we only see from one perspective and have one type of experience. This means we have a bias and we want to be able to let in all of the possible shapes so that we feel as though we are living rich and full lives, rather than dull and unsatisfactory lives.

Some people will find it helpful to understand the types of thoughts and match them to their own experience, such as catastrophising, personalising, black and white thinking, etc. For others, it's not necessary to categorise their 'warpy' thoughts. Either way, the thoughts get the better of you, and that is the root of stress in your mind which we want to eliminate. Do this process of capturing the thought for at least three days and then move onto the next step.

Some situations are like bad dreams, they're only unbearable while we're giving them our full attention. – Curtis Tyrone Jones

Altering the Mindscape – Reframing Thoughts

Now that you are more aware of your thoughts and understand what is going on in your mind and how it is affecting you, what do you do about it? The process begins now of actually beginning to alter the state of your mind. You may find yourself confronted with beliefs that you hold about yourself or stories you have been believing about the world that are simply holding you back or causing you to stay in fear, and you may notice your ego is in the driving seat. Such thoughts warp our reality and our behaviour that follows.

We need to strengthen your rational mind so that fears don't rule the show. Fears usually boil down to human needs such as wanting to be loved, accepted by others, and feel useful or a sense of belonging and purpose. Any threat to our sense of love and worthiness can become really inflated by the ego, which is just trying to protect us, but usually in an unhelpful way. We need to show it a better way.

To do this, refer back to the thought log you have been keeping and from now on, when you have a thought, jot it down and make a rational counter-statement. Begin by making counter-statements for the thoughts you have already written so that you get the hang of it. To use the example given before, a counter-statement of that may be: 'Xena is usually friendly to me and has not shown me any hostility before. I am confident that I have not upset her. I trust that she would tell me if I had. She hasn't, so I will accept that she did not see me or just wanted to eat lunch alone today – she probably has something on her mind that is not about me.'

The counter-statement is always rational in that it accepts the *evidence* of the situation (doesn't assume to know what others are thinking or feeling/mind-reading), is based in fact, is fair, and is humanitarian – it accepts that humans are not perfect, they are fallible, make mistakes, and that is ok as long as we learn from them and do better next time. It is usually optimistic too – it empowers you rather than disempowers. Generally, it conjures the opposite feelings of the other unhelpful thought.

An example could be: 'I know that when [name] doesn't answer their phone right away, that it is because they are simply busy. They will get back to me when they can, and they always do because they care about me. I can be patient and move on with my day whilst I await their response.'

Whenever you have a warped thought in future, capture it, and immediately create your rational counter-statement. Review this counter-statement as often as you need to and recite it *automatically* to yourself when its negative and unhelpful old version comes up. Through this process you unseat the thought, even if it's just a little, there's then a part of you that doesn't quite believe that thought.

Your worst enemy cannot harm you as much as your own thoughts unguarded – rule your mind or it will rule you. – Buddha

Take the Thought to Court and Put it on Trial

This can be done with any intrusive or negative and unhelpful thoughts that may enter your mind. A relatively simple yet powerful exercise you can do, either in your mind, speaking aloud, or on paper, is to imagine that you are the judge in a courtroom. The thought is on trial, and there is a lawyer in defence of the thought, and another in prosecution against the thought. Both lawyers present evidence for and against the truth of the thought and it is your job as judge to weigh the evidence, and ultimately assess the validity and decide whether you are going to allow the thought to continue to roam about in your mind, or turf it out for good. This sounds pretty straightforward but sometimes, simple is best, and some of my clients really find this way of looking at their thoughts very helpful as it allows you to step back from it.

Perhaps what you are experiencing though is not so much thoughts but images. You may find it helpful to play out this court scene with a 'still' or 'painting' of the unwanted image and have it sit on an easel in the room. Alternatively, as unwanted images enter your mind's eye, see them as if they were on a piece of paper and simply reach up, crumple the paper in your hand and toss it into a wastepaper basket. Do so as often as necessary, and eventually, the mind learns that communicating with you in that way is futile and it will happen less and less often.

Creating New Beliefs - Affirmations

Once you have gotten into the swing of creating your counter-statements and you have felt an emotional difference from repeating them to yourself after a worry or warped thought, your mind is now more receptive to new ideas – the soil of your mind has been tilled.

You may wish to turn your most-used counter-statements into affirmations that you repeat often or at least once a day for as long as you need to.

This is the classic process of learning through repetition, and eventually, your affirmations will become positive self-fulfilling beliefs. Affirmations are the 'I am's' that remain constant through the ever-changing seasons and situations of your life.

A really easy way to create a habit is to stack it onto an already existing habit. For affirmations, a great habit to stack it is to brushing your teeth. Not only do you already do this (I hope!) twice a day, but if you are doing it for two minutes each time, that's four minutes at least of repeating your affirmations *every* day. You can even list out your affirmations and time them to see if they do take two minutes to go through. Pen/type them up in a pleasing manner, frame them, and hang next to the sink where you brush your teeth. If you want them to remain private, then pop them in a plastic wallet and take them with you each time you brush your teeth. Intonate them in your head, and as you do so, really *feel* their meaning as true. You can even go through examples you have of the affirmation being true to really reinforce it. The more you do this, the easier it becomes to believe them as true.

I have different affirmations that I say for different times of the day. I have said three times *'A miracle is going to happen today'* every single morning since just before I was eighteen. This helped me to feel hopeful and somewhat taken care of. I also said every single night, *'Inside me is a golden glow, it lights the world around me, magick is within me, and it is in everything I see.'* I've said that for so long now I can't recall where I found it from, but it comforted me and allowed me to feel safe while I slept. I highly encourage you to find your own affirmations that become personal mantras. They can shift your mood and realign your focus.

Additionally, you can helpfully bombard yourself with the new things you want to believe by writing out counter-statements or affirmations on sticky-notes and dotting them around your home; when you open a cupboard: 'I am just as loveable as anyone else.' When you reach for a teabag: 'I don't need to do things perfectly to be a valuable human.' When you reach for your coat hanger: 'I provide value to my team at work.' You get the idea. You could also have little reminders pop up on your phone throughout the day of these affirmations. A fun thing to do is have a friend create and set them for you; that way, it really is a pleasant little reminder throughout your day. Your friend could even include little inside jokes or good memories too. Use this to your advantage so that it motivates and uplifts you throughout the day.

Worry is like walking around with an umbrella, waiting for it to rain.
– Wiz Khalifa

Challenge the Thoughts – Ask Yourself This

'Does it improve upon the silence?' At any point on the journey of getting your mind on your side, know that you are not your thoughts. You create your thoughts within your mind, and you can choose to not have them if you like, and you can choose to stop letting them control *you.* Our thoughts are spells that we are casting in our mind – they are not to be ignored.

A gentle way of challenging a thought if you can't think of how to create a direct counter-statement to it is to ask yourself if it improves upon the silence. This can stop a thought in its track, especially a thought-spiral, and give you some separation from the thoughts again. In that separation, you can then choose what to do next and choose a better thought that actually helps you on your journey to where you want to be and how you want to feel. You can then repeat mantras to yourself that describe positive feelings that you do want.

My philosophy is that worrying means you suffer twice. – Newt Scamander (Fantastic Beasts by J. K. Rowling)

Understanding Self-esteem – Nurturing Your Orchid

There are different facets that make up self-esteem, and it isn't to be confused with self-confidence. Confidence is situational and based on competency – you may be perfectly confident in one situation, such as performing team sports in front of thousands of on-lookers, but totally nervous and unconfident to give a speech in front of fifty people. Our level of comfort plays into confidence, which is why expanding our comfort zones and challenging ourselves with new things does increase confidence.

Self-esteem, on the other hand, is a continuum – it can rise and fall and is in a state of flow, which means it's something that needs to be continually nurtured and we need to be mindful of it. If we do something we are not confident with and it goes well, we often experience an increase to our self-esteem because we have a new situation we can trust ourselves in, a new situation to believe in our abilities with; we may praise ourselves and accept compliments and recognise how challenging that was but did it anyway. Yet if we do something and it goes poorly, and then we also berate ourselves harshly and unhelpfully about the outcome of the situation, and we can easily damage our self-esteem.

The primary facets to self-esteem then are self-belief, self-trust, self-respect, self-compassion, self-worth and self-love, and I like to imagine them as petals on a flower with a self-esteem-pollen centre. When you start looking at the details of these components, you are likely to realise how complex self-esteem is and how it very much is an internal orchid that needs to be cared for if we are to be mentally healthy and feel well in general.

I encourage you now to pop this book down and take a few moments to let this sink in; really let it permeate around with you for a bit, and consider the primary facets. If the facets are petals to your orchid, how would they each actually look – would they be healthy? Why or why not? Get clear on this because I guarantee it will serve you moving forwards. How might you be damaging the petals, or what is hurting them currently? What changes can you implement to nurture each petal? What beliefs are limiting you in each area? This allows you to zoom into self-esteem and helps you identify with more clarity why it may be lower than you'd like.

Building Self-esteem – Recognise Your Achievements

If you ever struggle to take a compliment or find yourself focusing on the one thing you believed you could have done better, rather than the ninety-nine other things you did excellently, there are two major things you can do to shift this mode of thinking.

Every time someone compliments you for whatever reason, say 'thank you'. Just that. Forget about the niggle in the back of your head that might think they have an agenda behind their compliment or believes they said it to be nice because they feel sorry for you, etc. Just say 'thank you'. Let the compliment soak in. It feels weird to do this at first. It may feel strange the first 100 times you do this, but eventually, it starts to feel nice, maybe even a little 'glowy' and warm. Do as previously discussed with rationalising and counter-statements with the 'warpy' or unhelpful thoughts that may pop in after hearing the compliment, but in that moment, accept the compliment graciously with a smile and a 'thank you'.

Secondly, keep a log of each compliment you receive and any achievement you have earnt. You can start this log by writing some historical achievements that you are proud of and then continue this log from there. If you receive the same compliment, you could simply keep a tally next to where it is already written on your list. You'll likely come to a point where you no longer feel the need to continue with this log. You will know you have then really begun to heal a part of you that believes that you are not worthy or unlovable. This log can then serve as a reminder that you do have worth and do have successes, and it can be added into your wellness/self-love toolbox for when you need that reminder.

Time is a created thing. To say 'I don't have time' is like saying, 'I don't want to.' – Lao Tzu

Handling Decision Fatigue/Decision Paralysis

Every decision and choice require mental energy, and sometimes emotional energy as well if the subject is evocative or complicated around people's lives and feelings. And sometimes, when we have a lot going on – maybe we're feeling stressed, overwhelmed or just tired, and our self-care is perhaps not as good as it could be – we need a simple solution to actually help us make decisions so that we actually are moving in some direction.

Decision fatigue is more when you don't have the energy to make decisions, weigh up consequences, etc. This is usually noticed through having trouble with the 'bigger' decisions where there needs to be some weighing-up of the larger picture, consequences, pros and cons. Decision paralysis is more like an inability to make any decision; there's an element of fear there too, and it often links to low self-esteem. This operates more so with simple decisions, like when someone asks you if you would like a cup of tea and your response is to smile and shrug or say 'I don't mind', and that happens *a lot.*

For those of you who are faced with a type of decision issue, you may find it helpful to make a list of different things you could do that day, or whatever choices it is you are between, or with the list prompts throughout this book. If when you look at the list, nothing jumps out at you as the definite thing you want to do or choose, you may find it initially helpful to take away some of that onus of making a decision. You could number each point on the list and roll a dice or two, or use a random number generator and take the corresponding action. If you have no dice or technology to hand, then good old '*eenie, meenie, miney, mo*' can work! If it is two decisions and you're with someone, chatting to someone online or on the phone, you may ask them to assign each thing to either their left or right hand. When they tell you they're done, then you choose either their left or right, or close your eyes and tap one of their fists if they're with you in-person and holding their hands in front of you. Whichever you land on is what you do. That works well for simple choices such as which film to watch or what to eat.

With all of these methods, the idea isn't to be at mercy to 'fate'; it's to notice that immediate feeling you have to the outcome that is presented to you. If you make a mind map of all activities you enjoy and you swirl your finger about over the paper with your eyes closed and point, and whatever you land on, you feel a pang of disappointment … you know you didn't actually want to do that thing. Then you have learnt something, eliminated something, and can choose again until you get to the pang of joy or excitement because you're now doing something that you want.

The aim is to strengthen the part of you that notices what you want or need so that you can listen to it. Then you'll be acting from a place of more authenticity, and that is good for your wellness and happiness. In time, hopefully, as your understanding of yourself deepens, you'll be able to more wisely choose an action that would be the most beneficial in the circumstances. As you build trust in your ability to make decisions, making them becomes easier, but you need to start, and you can start somewhere simple! Starting is the hard part, but once you do and you have a few strategies that work for you, you build on that initial momentum and keep building on it until one day you notice it's no longer a problem for you.

Alongside this, you may like to see where in your life you are making unnecessary decisions. Take yesterday to start with and write down, from each moment, all the decisions you made from the time you woke up until you woke up today. What are some simple things that you honestly spent too long deciding on or that were hard, despite being simple things in the grand scheme? This could be things relating to food and cooking meals or fixing snacks, or outfit choices or other things in your 'getting ready' routine, or even what to watch or read. With any of these too-long or too-hard decisions that really should be simpler, take the time now to mind-map some ways that you could actually make these simpler in the day-to-day of your life. Internet-search some solutions if you need to, or 'hacks' – there's bound to be some help for whatever it is, and you can always ask a friend for ideas if you're stuck. Chances are they have the issue too and would like to work it out, and you're presenting them with the opportunity to, or they don't struggle with that and can offer you how they work it out.

Some examples that I've done in the past which have helped are: decluttering my stuff, especially clothing, accessories, personal-care items and kitchenware regularly so that I know what is there I like, feel good in, or have use for. Breaking my wardrobe into seasons and rotating it, so I know that what I'm choosing from fits the weather, which naturally means there's less visual choice, which feels less overwhelming in itself because I've already thought about what I like to wear in that season upfront and made deciding easier on future-me. Meal planning also works well for a lot of people, and things like checking the fridge for what needs using up so they can plan their lunch or make it ready for tomorrow so that when they are there, tomorrow, looking in the fridge and hungry, they have already made that decision.

All of these things are also about being mindful of your energy (remember the teapot analogy from earlier on) and taking that time to understand yourself, and then take those small little actions that don't really take much effort now, but have a big and helpful impact on you in the future. Aren't you happy at past-you for being so nice to future-you (which is really current-you)!? Let's make the answer *yes*!

Anxiety is one little tree in your whole forest. Step back and look at the whole forest. – Unknown

Understand the Nature of Anxiety for You

Sometimes we realise anxiety has no immediate reason for being there but it sort of has become a constant. This was my experience of generalised anxiety. Whilst sometimes there are obvious build-ups or triggers, sometimes there just aren't, and you're always in a heightened state. Anxiety can be insidious like that; for example, it may only happen when walking on your own and then it starts to spread to when you're in the car on your own too. Understand this is part of the mechanism of anxiety. It makes us uncomfortable, so we don't put ourselves in 'scary' situations, even if there's nothing logically there to be afraid of or no real danger.

It can only take one moment and then a period of stress for anxiety to become your body's way of trying to keep you safe because of that one time you listened to the anxiety. The problem is it makes you live small by shrinking your comfort zone, and we don't want to live small, yet all of a sudden it's hard because now you feel anxious doing something that wasn't previously an issue for you.

Look back. Was the thing that you now experience anxiety over always an anxious occurrence for you? Looking back like this can help you find the courage to tell the anxiety you don't need it anymore. Realise that it may once have served a purpose but that you no longer need the sense of dread and accompanying tummy ache. Thank it for warning you and tell it goodbye if it starts to creep up.

Rapidly Diminish a State of Panic – Box Breathing

This is an extremely powerful body-to-mind technique for calming you whenever anxiety becomes strong.

Close your eyes and whilst breathing in for a count of four, you imagine drawing the top side of a square, then hold your breath for a count of four and visualise drawing the down side of the square.

Next, breathe out for a count of four and draw the bottom of your square.

Lastly, hold your empty lung space for a count of four and draw the other side of the square to meet where you started. Repeat until you feel calm again, and if you like, you can increase the counts up to ten and go back down to four – by then you should feel utterly relaxed.

This works by forcing the brain to re-evaluate where it is sending oxygenated blood, making it go back towards your organs rather than the muscles in your limbs, because when experiencing anxiety, physiologically the body is in flight-fight-freeze mode (your sympathetic nervous system is activated) – blood rushes to your limbs which can increase feelings of pain in the chest area, which is very common to feel with panic.

Your mind is also occupied drawing your square or box and with counting, which is a non-threatening activity, so we are telling your brain to calm down and put your body back into rest-digest-restore mode (parasympathetic nervous system). Really make this yours; I have had *Potterhead* clients who imagine it as a glowing Patronus square! Do what captivates you best.

Men are disturbed not by things, but by the views they take of them.

– *Epictetus*

'Fear of a Name Increases Fear of the Thing Itself'

You may recognise that as a quote from Albus Dumbledore if you've read the *Harry Potter* books (or Hermione Granger said it in the films); and the author, Joanne, is right. A huge part of my role within psychotherapy is to help my clients externalise their problems and fears. Sometimes, we unknowingly attach the fear/issue to be a part of our identity, and we may need a method to start seeing it as something separate and external to us. This can even be the case with obsessive thoughts that intrude into our mind and generate negative emotions. When we externalise it, we're able to exert control over it as it becomes something we can influence.

A way of externalising it is to give whatever it is a name. Maybe it already has a name, for example, if you have received a diagnosis or have developed a name for whatever it is already in your head. The next step would be to assign features to it: make it humanoid, an entity or even a monster - make it 'other' somehow. To continue with the *HP* reference, you could see it as a boggart. See it as a separate part of you – external. How does it operate? Does it 'visit' sometimes, or it is more like a parasite, and if it is, where does it attach? Then make it *riddikulus* (like the spell in *Harry Potter)*! Dress it up in silly clothes, whatever's funny to you. Laughter is the opposite of fear, so use it wherever you can.

Whenever the thoughts, feelings or impulses that this thing creates occur, notice them and remember these are being generated by the thing and you can choose to not accept them. You can graciously and assertively tell them to go away or ride the wave and let them fade, turn to a safe action, reach out to a safe person instead. This may be easier said than done, but practice does make perfect, and externalising and not acting as the thing wants you to does get easier with time.

Another way to externalise something is to get curious about it. Whenever you notice the feeling or thought pop up, simply witness it and as if it were an unexpected stranger who has knocked at your door, ask them questions – 'What is it you're here to tell me?' 'What do you need in order to be on your merry way?' You can question the stranger at the door – you do not have to invite them in. You are most unlikely to invite a perfect stranger into your home, especially one that carried negativity with them! Apply this approach to any intrusive thought in your mind.

Mind Your Language – Abracadabra

Abracadabra is one of those words it seems every child knows – it's a fun word to say! It's an Aramaic (before Hebrew) phrase from 'avara kehdabra' which literally means, 'I will create as I speak.' Let's face it - the spoken word has been around far longer than the written word. We allude to the power of spoken words through common parlance like 'their *command* of language'. That very phrase is directional and points to the fact that words do give you a certain power.

Writing is powerful, but speaking is not to be overlooked either. A witch knows the added effect of rhyme. How the rhythm of a rhyming verse precedes its written form. Memory psychologists and the like note the added benefit of rhymes as an aid memoir and we can all remember certain nursery rhymes from childhood.

So, be aware of the language you use around how you feel and what you experience. Are you attaching yourself to something and therefore integrating it as part of your identity: *my anxiety, my fear, my depression, I am overwhelmed, I am angry*? There's a difference between accepting there is an issue and owning it in the sense that you recognise you have control ultimately, and over-attaching to something so that it becomes part of the filter through which you think about and see yourself. Putting 'I am' before anything you don't want makes it an affirmation nonetheless.

It is more helpful in the long-term to use language that externalizes the condition to you: 'the anxiety I have experienced', 'the depression that sometimes visits me', 'stress is here'. This recognises that the emotion is not ever-present/constant and removes it from becoming a part of your identity. It is not you, you are not it – separate it from you.

Noticing the emotion, breathing, labelling the emotion, and continuing to breathe is mindfulness in action, which can help you separate from the emotion so that you learn from it, but then chose how to proceed rather than have the emotion rule you.

I will not let anyone walk through my mind with their dirty feet.
– Mahatma Gandhi

AIR ~ PART II
SO BELOW

The ancestor of every action is a thought.
– Ralph Waldo Emerson

***

Get to Know Your Mind and Body – Pattern Tracking

Sometimes we can hinder our recovery by not looking holistically at our lives. For some people, while they're really working on gaining control over the anxiety they experience, they benefit from cutting down on unnecessary caffeine or sugar, for example, because they are stimulants. Other people though won't really find a relationship between their experience with anxiety or negative mood and foods or substances, such as tobacco.

If you do suspect something you feed your body or mind with is impairing your sense of wellbeing, you can begin a process of slowly decreasing that substance or thing (such as your phone) from your day and tracking how you feel. After a couple of weeks, it will become clear whether you feel any better for not having so much of that substance or thing. Seek support for this if you choose this process as you do not want it to be an unnecessarily stressful experience for you – it should feel slightly liberating!

Getting to know your body can be really helpful in getting to the root of anxiousness, low mood, and irritability. Food allergies/intolerance, hormonal (especially menstruating females), nutritional, and thyroid problems can all trigger difficult mood symptoms. Understanding your body's natural tendencies can lead to freedom. You may want to work with a doctor, dietitian, gynaecologist, or psychotherapist to understand these potential causes if you suspect they may be contributing to your state of wellness.

There are many tracker apps and templates for different things available online, so you're sure to find something that works for you. As a soon-to-be married woman, I reflected on why I was taking hormonal birth control. I had tried many different types and doses, and they would be okay at first, but then I would get horrible side-effects. I didn't believe that I would naturally have problems with my menstrual cycle, as I never did before I went on birth control. So, after discussion with my partner and gynaecologist, I chose to no longer be on hormonal birth control. I focus my personal charting around my 'Moon cycle', as it's affectionately called (see resources section), and note other things on top of that which I always record, such as Moon phase, general daily mood and motivation, exercise type and meditation type, and anything else I am choosing to keep a particular eye on at that time. Doing this also helps because if there is an issue, you have already documented evidence to present to your doctor if necessary.

Man is not worried about real problems so much as by his imagined anxieties about real problems. – Epictetus

Free Your Mind of Worry and Clutter – Thought Dump

You may identify as being a worrier, like I used to be, where you feel as though you can't switch off from worrying or you ruminate on a thought, seemingly endlessly, and jump into the future with 'what-if' scenarios. This is a massive drain of emotional and mental energy and soon starts to sap at your sense of wellbeing. Worry can really be a burden and definitely can create feelings of anxiety and stress, which can affect concentration, sleep, and your immune system. However, worry isn't inherently a negative feeling – sometimes it can alert us that something needs attention, and motivate us to take positive action or find ways to avoid undesired outcomes and plan for the future. Yet it is seldom used so constructively.

Alternatively, you may be someone who feels that their mind is heavy with clutter or drifts to judging the present. In either case, the following will be helpful for you too, because just as when we want to invite something new into our lives, we clear out the old, we do the same with our mind. How can we expect to have an abundance of helpful thoughts when we have reams of unhelpful ones in the way?

The best place to start with that I have found myself and with many clients is to do a thought dump. It works well first thing in the morning because you give your mind chance to run amok and then you have all day to take action if necessary. However, you may find it more helpful before bed – do what is most effective for you. If you're doing this to help with worry, set a timer for as long as you feel you need to worry. Either way, write down everything that is in your head that is a concern or worry. Get it out. Put it in black and white. Empty everything – it doesn't matter if it doesn't make sense, or if it's not spelt correctly or in sentences; it doesn't need to be perfect, you just need to get it out of your head and onto the paper.

Do this in a space where it is okay to worry. Do not do this in a place you want to feel calm, such as in your bed – better to sit on the floor or in a chair you don't go in any other time. You don't want to start associating a space you want to feel productive, creative, or relaxed in with worry.

Optional step: Close your eyes and visualise everything you have written in a pile in front of you. Now see yourself standing up, growing ever taller until you grow so tall you're a giant and towering over the building you were just in, the area you just were. You're so high up now, you're with the birds flying in the clear sky. Look how small your pile is, you can barely even make it out! Notice how good that feels, to be up there, not bothered by these things … Open your eyes.

Set a further timer for at least ten minutes and spend that time assessing each thing you have written down and apply Socratic questioning to it:

~What is the evidence for/against this thought?

~Is it based in fact, or on feelings?

~Am I assuming emotions are evidence of facts?

~Is it black and white or is reality more complex?

~Am I making assumptions/mind-reading on someone?

~Do other people have a different point of view on this situation – what are they?

~Is this thought an exaggeration or minimisation of the truth?

~Am I imposing a standard onto someone else they 'should know' they are being held to, but they really don't?

~Am I jumping to conclusions with this thought?

~What do my thoughts and feelings about this issue tell me about my belief of myself, others, and the world?

~Am I dismissing the positives in this situation?

~Am I over-emphasising the negatives of this situation?

~Did someone pass this thought/belief to me – are they a reliable source for this?

~Is it a likely scenario or worst case – what can I do about this?

~If it really were to happen – can I survive – how could I cope? (Come up with a contingency plan.)

~If I look at this positively, how is it different?

~Am I overestimating the probability something bad might happen – is my concern realistic?

~Is it a real problem or an imaginary 'what if'?

~Is it about something I need to do or is it from a defensive point – is it my ego coming in to play?

~What is a more balanced way to look at this?

~If a loved one had this worry, what would I tell them?

~Will this matter next week? Will it matter in a month? In three months? In six months? A year from now? Is it worth the anguish to worry about this now if it won't matter soon?

~Is there anything I can action straight away (perhaps a phone call to make or email you need to send)?

~Anything I can get done today and off this page so that it's done and out of my head? (Diarise this).

~For the thoughts that I've written, do they actually help or serve me at all?

~If I've had a strong negative reaction to something about someone else's behaviour/something they've done, is it because they have broken one of my 'rules'? If yes, have I calmly, respectfully, and assertively communicated this rule as a boundary to them and did we have a conversation about this? If I realise this rule is unreasonable and causing myself and others pain in some way, can I choose to accept it and let it go?

~If I feel bad or guilty, is it because I've 'broken' some sort of rule that I believe governs me in some way?

~Is there anything I need to make a counter-statement for, anything that is a 'warpy' belief or thought? Write the counter-statement.

If you conclude the worry you're having is unhelpful and unnecessary, make the decision to stop having it. Put any stubbornness you may have to good use and discipline your mind. If any worry pops up outside of this scheduled worry time, notice it, tell it to stop, that it is not the time and it is to go away – you will address it at the next scheduled thought dump. Remind yourself *'I am in control of my thoughts'* and choose to only focus on thoughts that serve you.

You may find yourself clinging to a need to control, like I often found that I was. I kidded myself into believing that if I had every eventuality covered, then everything would be better. What actually happened was the joy was sapped from a lot of things, and they lost their sparkle because I couldn't be in the moment – in the now – truly present. Anxiety wasn't coming from thinking of the future (that should be a positive experience); it came from wanting to control it. Our arrow points to whatever we focus on, but just as the wind can influence the path of the arrow, there are many factors influencing the course of your plans. You cannot control everything – some things are uncertain. That's one of the reasons divination was so appealing at first; however, knowing things didn't actually bring me any peace – I'd just find something else to worry about!

If you're not present, you're not in joy, you're not in the flow of life, and you're definitely not in the flow of love. Magick is in the moment, and that magick can't happen if you're squeezing something so tight it can't breathe. That goes for mundane things too!

Acknowledge any discomfort, know that it's okay, you will survive it, then choose to focus your attention onto the things you can influence. We're too often so predisposed with not feeling uncomfortable that we forget it won't last forever, that in life, every state is temporary, and so we fear the uncomfortable – avoid, run away, distract from, numb out … Remember to stay present – do not future-trip or revisit the past for negative reasons. Remember where you are and that you are okay (or better than okay).

Find peace with the things you cannot change. Thank the worry for alerting you and trying to keep you safe, let it know you can handle the situation or that there is nothing you can do right now, that you're open to solutions as they present themselves, send it love and let it go.

Once you have crossed out things you have concluded are not worth worrying about, problem-solve with what remains. These should be specific things that you know exactly why and how you're worried about them. You should be as clear as possible about this:

~How can you solve this issue? Write the solution down.

~Do you need more information on it before you can find a solution – plan how you will do this and when.

~Do you need to ask someone for assistance?

~Is there anything you can do to lessen the impact of this concern?

~What is the next step you can take? Plan time to do this.

Commit to this practice at the same time every day if you can. This makes it easier to let worries go that may pop up outside of allotted worry time because you can assure yourself that you *will* be giving the thought some time tomorrow and know that to be true. Over time, you should find you need to spend less and less minutes on the thought dump, and long-term, you should find you naturally problem solve straight away in your daily life and action things so they don't become a worry or immediately have a rational belief about something that would have, in the past, caused you a worry or to ruminate.

You wouldn't worry so much about what other think of you if you realized how seldom they do. – Eleanor Roosevelt

Changing Your Self-story - Reframing Emotions

An effective technique within neuro-linguistic programming is understanding the physiological (brain and body) patterns that occur with different emotions and then account what you are feeling to a more helpful emotion that uses the same physiological patterns. A useful example is *nerves* and *excitement.* Both have exactly the same physiological symptoms (increased heart rate and breathing, uncomfortable stomach, shaking, sweating, etc.), so if your mind notices these symptoms and labels them as nerves, you could feel, for example, disempowered, uncomfortable, or self-conscious. However, if you were to label the sensations you notice as excitement, you could feel optimistic and confident. I encourage you to learn more about what goes on in your body with a particular emotion. You can do so by reflecting on your personal experience and then researching the physiology to explain why you feel what you do with that emotion. This gives your rational mind more power and enables you to understand the sensations such that you can re-label them with a helpful emotion in future.

Challenge Yourself – Expand Your Comfort Zone

You may be aware of the things that you used to find easy but seem now so difficult or scary. Remember that anxiety by its very nature shrinks your comfort zone, often without you realising it is happening. One of the most powerful things you can do to start freeing yourself of the hold anxiety can have over you is to start facing that which brings feelings of anxiety or fear and actually challenge them head-on.

Once you have a few tools that work for you that you can use within a moment if you need to and before doing something, so that you can calm yourself and approach the task with as clear of a mind as you can, then it may be time to begin the process of re-expanding your comfort zone.

You will likely know when you are ready for this. It feels a little frightening to think about the task you're looking to try, but you feel up for the challenge and ready to let yourself try.

You can do this yourself, with the support of someone trustworthy, or with a professional, such as a therapist, and these fear-challenges could be your therapy goals. Begin by having your end goal – it may be something like going ice-skating by yourself, or going to the supermarket and chatting to the checkout clerk. An example for me was driving without having someone else in the car with dual-controls – a thought that made me feel very ill and gave me nightmares.

With whatever it is you'd like to be able to do, write down the smaller steps you're going to need to go through to reach your end goal. Decide what is realistic and what pace is manageable. It may be that you take one small step towards your goal a day, or it may be more feasible to do one a week. Challenging yourself and facing your fears is a fantastic and sure-fire way to raise your confidence and trust in yourself.

Many people start to build momentum to this, and it becomes fun to work on challenging their fears! If/when that becomes you, you can plan to do one new thing every day or one thing that's a little scary every day to keep you expanding, experiencing, and learning about yourself.

I did then what I knew how to do. Now that I know better, I do better.
– Maya Angelou

Create an Anchor – the 'Muggle' Patronus

An anchor is a classical conditioning technique that works with stimulus-response psychology and helps you diminish fear or panic and steady yourself, much like the anchor of a boat. It can combat the feeling you don't want and is created similarly to a Patronus in *J. K. Rowling's Wizarding World.* It's easy to use; play around with the technique and find what works best for you.

First, you need to think of a memory: a time, place or event in your life which has no negative emotion connected to it. A time when you were at peace, content and happy. Not excited-happy, like on a roller-coaster, as we're trying to bring energy *down*. A content and peaceful happiness is what you're looking for. Try to find a memory that has a lot of sensory information with it: sights, sounds, smells, tastes, and touch. Asking your brain to activate all five sensory fields requires more areas of the brain to be used in reproducing the memory, leaving less of the brain to focus on trauma, anxiety, panic, or fear.

If all of your happy memories are tainted with fear, pain, or other negative emotions, you might want to use a fantasy instead. If you have a more emotionally satisfying memory that only uses three senses and it works to calm you down much better than one which uses all five senses – use it.

What is most important is that it is a beautiful, *calm* and *happy* memory for you and that it works to lessen any anxiety or fear felt.

Once you have your happy memory, move through the senses it evokes one at a time and try to relive them:

What do you *see*?

What do you *hear*?

What do you *smell*?

What do you *taste*?

What do you *feel*?

Now, sit with that memory for as long as you like or need to. When the memory of the desired state is at its strongest, 'anchor' it in by making the physical gesture you want to use for that desired state. For example, you might touch your thumb and middle finger together and say to yourself, 'I am calm.'

Hold the feeling of the desired state for a moment while you continue to make the anchor gesture, then release the gesture and immediately change your thoughts to something very different: maybe what your pet is doing, what type of tea you'd like to make next, what may happen next in your book or TV show, or outside the window …

Repeat this process up to ten times in order to create a strong anchor, and do so as often as necessary. When you think you're finished creating the anchor, be sure to test it by 'casting it'. Ensure that you actually enter the desired state. If it doesn't seem to be working, try to repeat the anchor creation process or consider using a different, stronger memory.

Use it whenever you need it to decrease anxiety or help calm you to sleep. Change it in whatever way you need to in order for it to be most effective for you.

You can also create anchors for different emotional states, such as confidence. Tie each emotional state to a unique anchor and gesture that you can 'cast' when needed.

There is also the option to create an anchor to a scent. This is actually how I created my first anchor with lavender, and it was during my undergraduate while participating in a research study, interested in aromatherapy and mood. Firstly, pick an essential oil that is skin safe (or made skin safe by mixing with a carrier oil, see resource section), that either has no current meaning for you or already has a desired effect on you.

In this example, we will use relaxation. Take time out every day for a week to form the anchor, except instead of using the gesture, you breathe in the scent. As you breathe, conjure the feeling of total relaxation. Do this for between one and five minutes. After this week, whenever you start to feel anxious, nervous or anything where you'd rather feel calm, take out your little pipet or ball-roller bottle of oil and apply a few drops to the back of your wrists and breathe it in deeply.

If the anchor works, you should feel calmer and relaxed. This works really well for me as I have a strong response to scents (stronger than the gesture anchor, in fact). Note that the reason this is with an oil and not a perfume is because perfumes are layered with notes of different scents and wear too differently depending on the time of day, heat, and what's chemically going on with your skin, so it's not as reliable as a straight-up, plain essential oil.

This principle can be applied to strengthen your magickal or other workings. If you always pair the same scents and sounds to a particular activity or mental or emotional state, then whenever you want to get into that state in the future, simply having the presence of the scent or sound can help you get into that state quicker and easier. This can be useful with, for example, getting into the ritual mindset, signalling sleepiness, focus, or a feeling of energy. Practitioners may have clothing that they reserve specifically for working magick and so that signals to their unconscious the intention that they are going into a ritual. All things like this act as a cue to our unconscious that a particular state is going to follow. It almost acts as a gateway on a path, but instead of the path's gate being closed, it's already open. Use this to your advantage.

People become attached to their burdens sometimes more than burdens are attached to them. – George Bernard Shaw

Become More Present – Mindfulness Meditation

The positive things you'll learn with mindfulness will have space to take root in your mind when it is a little less chaotic and crowded if you are struggling. Mindfulness essentially teaches you how to let go of thoughts and emotions, acknowledge them, yes, but not react to them. There's a balance between feeling so you can be in touch with emotions – because they are the information from what's going on both within us and outside of us – and rationality. Logic to the exclusion of emotion is of no use to humans and makes them cold to themselves and others.

Mindfulness is also known as the middle path because you walk with one foot in rationality and another in emotionality to find a balance of wisdom between them. You have to feel to heal, so this isn't about ignoring emotion, dismissing it or squashing it entirely with logic. It's about acknowledging the feelings in a way that is healthy and helpful to you, and part of that means not reacting on an overwhelming emotion, getting carried away with it and then regretting how things went because you did not temper yourself. Temperance is part of wise mind – the middle path. Mindfulness teaches that you already have an imperturbable mind and helps you regain your state of wellness if your mind does become perturbed. When the mind feels well, it tends to act well. Meditation is a mental muscle and so must be practised regularly to feel all of the true and full benefits from it.

It is also about being in the present and only in the present, making it a wonderful tool for those struggling with anxiousness, worry, dwelling, anger, or general future-tripping. Not to say that thinking of the future is a bad thing: of course it isn't, it's very necessary. However, spending too much time in the future can be a sign that you're mentally running away from things in the present, or simply spending time agonising over possibilities and not actually putting contingency plans in place and trusting in them, others, and yourself so that you aren't in worry.

This can also be said of spending too much time thinking of the past, reminiscing on how things were to the detriment of your present life; or feeling dissatisfied with something that happened and dwelling on it over and over again, to the point where you're basically torturing yourself if you're being honest.

If this at all sounds like you, a good rule of thumb for a day is spending 80% of your time thinking of the present, 10%

of your thoughts reflecting and learning so you can evolve and move forwards, and 10% thinking of the future so you can plan and dream big!

When practised regularly, it increases the space between having the thought and then your *action* because of that thought, or action because of a feeling you have noticed. You proceed through your life with a greater sense of purpose and peace and develop more compassion, rather than being at the mercy of your surroundings and mind. If your mind is alive with the present, there is no room for the past.

There are many great apps now that teach you mindfulness meditation, as well as audiobooks, reading books, online and in-person courses. If you don't get on with the first one you try, I encourage you to find another you do get on with, as we all learn differently and I'm confident you'll find a style that works for you if you search for it.

I believe that mindfulness meditation was one of the best things I have ever taken the time to learn and *everyone* else I know who has immersed into it has greatly benefitted from it, as it is so versatile and helpful in every-day life. It has a *lot* of empirical support, and its principles are fundamental or paralleled to respected therapeutic approaches such as dialectical behaviour therapy, acceptance and commitment therapy, and person-centred therapy.

Meditation is mindfulness in practice, and it helps you change your relationship between what you think and feel and what you are. You realise you're not what you think and feel; you are just a witness to experience.

Be careful of the thought-seeds that you plant in the garden of your mind. – Funkadelic

Let Go Charm

Sometimes we need a little extra support that helps to steer us in the right direction and let go of emotions that have done their job of informing us about what is going on. Allow calming herbs and crystals to assist you with this.

You'll need at least two types of dried herbs/flowers that are calming to you, for example, camomile (great for calming as well as balance as it represents the Sun and the Moon) and lavender (renowned to be relaxing and soothing), and some calming crystals such as blue calcite, lapis lazuli, blue lace agate, or amethyst.

Cast a circle if you like and use spell components (like incense) that signal calm to you.

When you yourself feel calm and centred, draw out a symbol or create a sigil (see page 165 for sigil creation) that signifies calm to you.

Once you're happy with your design, paint, draw or stitch it onto a cloth pouch or bag.

In a little dish, stir the herbs together with your finger clockwise and keep the feeling of calm going until you feel ready to pop the herbs into the pouch along with your chosen crystals.

Carry this charm with you to help remind you to let go and help assist you with any mindfulness, meditation, or manifestation practices that you may be doing.

Now that years have passed, I recall my troubles and wonder that they could distress me so much. It will be the same thing, too, with this trouble. Time will go by and I shall not mind about this either.
– Leo Tolstoy

Spellcraft - Make a Thought Braid or Catcher

This is a simple craft and can be done in different sizes, lengths, and with as many strands as you are able to braid or want to. For example, you could use embroidery thread and make a bracelet for yourself, or ribbon and make something to hang where you'll see it often. What you use to braid with, how many strands, and where it will be displayed is up to you.

You will need a minimum of three colours for this craft – one to represent you, and at least two others to represent your new mindset. To illustrate, I would personally use purple to represent myself, green to represent self-love and forgiveness, and white to symbolise patience. As I want to grow these things, I would perform this on a waxing Moon on a Friday because I associate that day with love, which feels appropriate for my intention.

During your chosen Moon phase, take your chords and secure them somewhere so that you can braid easily (I knot them at the top and trap them in a closed drawer so I can pull them tight enough to make a neat braid).

You can cast a circle if you like or set the mood with appropriate scents, candles, etc. for your purpose, and when you're focused and clear on your intention, begin the braid.

While braiding, think of you being more of the qualities you desire and feel into that; chant the words as you do so if you like.

Once your braid is finished, you may tie it appropriately or decorate it further with charms that echo the intention, close the circle and wear or display your craft.

Another great form of this spellcraft is to make a dreamcatcher in the same manner, except rather than it catching your good dreams, it catches your intended qualities or new mindset.

Self-help – Emotional Freedom Technique (EFT)

If you struggle with shame or self-judgement, you may find some relief by practising EFT. It's a mind-to-body technique that gently helps you to think in a different way and release the emotions or thoughts that are holding you back, working on the principle that we can hold emotions and memories physically in our body.

It's not for everyone, but as with all of these practices, it's worth giving a go as you never know! YouTube is a great resource for tapping videos you can follow along to. Simply type your key word of the issue, or thing you want more of (e.g. joy) and then EFT to find a relevant video.

Your mind is for having ideas, not holding them.
– David Allen

The Power of Lucid Dreaming and a Dreaming Ritual

I became interested in the theories of dreams and dream symbolism initially. My curiosity led me to lucid dreaming, which was then the gateway for how I developed an interest in psychology, as it led me to Sigmund Freud from his theories on the unconscious mind. Lucid dreaming in itself is not only a fun skill to perform, but it also has mental health and magickal benefits.

In terms of mental health, it is infinitely useful if you are someone who has problematic nightmares. Once you learn to lucid dream, you will always have the ability to face your fears within the dream and change the ending for how you want it to go. This is a hugely empowering skill. One of the theories of dreams is that they sometimes serve as preparations for things our mind fears we will encounter in waking life. By presenting us with scenarios in our dreams, we have the chance to safely practise facing these challenges, problem-solving and overcoming them, so that if a similar situation should happen in waking life, we will handle it better.

This is nice of our mind, sure, but it doesn't make it any less scary in the dream, and it can unsettle us for a long time when we do wake. Lucid dreaming would allow you to have more control in the dream, even though you are still sleeping, and because with lucid dreaming you realise you are dreaming but don't wake up, you have the chance to decide to face the situation head-on. This can increase your self-confidence, self-belief, and courage.

As for witching, most witches and spiritual manifestors will know the power of visualisation, feeling and acting 'as if'. Therefore, intentional lucid dreaming really allows you the chance to fully experience a desire. Because the brain isn't brilliant at discerning a dream experience from a real experience, you would be playing out your preferred scenario as if it really is the case (as far as your brain is concerned anyway). If you have ever woken to feel the physical effects of a dream – perhaps you woke crying, laughing or in pain somewhere relating to what happened in the dream – then this may definitely be something for you to try as it would seem you already connect your physical self very strongly to your dreams.

There is a lot of help now for how you can teach yourself to lucid dream (see resource section) and with any of the suggestions in this book I strongly recommend you do your own research first before using. I already could lucid dream, most likely because I'm a light sleeper and light sleepers have been shown to have more of the hormone norepinephrine, which is related to memory, and thus more easily remember the vivid and emotive dreams experienced during REM sleep (rapid-eye-movement) which is when dreams occur. I didn't know I was lucid dreaming initially, which is likely to be the case for many magickal people; but in order to get even better at lucid dreaming, a trick is to understand your typical dream-scapes and symbolism so that you recognise it as elements of your personal dream world and thus know you are not awake.

The easiest way to do this is to keep a notepad and pencil by your bed so that as soon as you wake you can scribble about the dream in as much detail as possible, preferably before you open your eyes and let the material world in. The more you do this, the more you will teach yourself about your dream worlds, and the easier it becomes for you to recognise a dream when it is happening. Writing them down is also good for seeing what your subconscious is up to.

The below simple ritual is something I use when I want to increase the likelihood that I will lucid dream that night.

It will start with having a strong night-time routine in which you are focusing on resting, relaxing and setting the intention to dream that night.

You may like to have a herbal tea infused with plants that are especially reported to aid in dreaming, but you will most likely want to experiment and see what works best for you. My personal blend is on page 63. All of these are pretty easy to get hold of for most people or to grow their own.

If you're not into drinking tea, just have your normal bedtime drink and perhaps craft a dried herb sachet of these plants to place by your pillow instead and draw on it a dreaming sigil (see page 165 for sigil creation).

Enhance the relaxation further by applying a lavender or camomile scented hand cream or body lotion. Do your necessary preparations for the next day and ensure that before you have your drink, you are ready for sleep so that you can essentially finish it, then brush your teeth, and then go straight to sleep. Whatever your beverage, light an appropriately scented candle or use a candle fuelled oil-burner and watch the candle as you sip the drink, focusing on your intent to lucid dream. This should feel almost meditative.

Once you have finished the drink, don't delay with going to sleep as soon as possible. When you lay down and are comfortable, if you are going to be using the dream time for more magickal purposes, go to sleep visualising yourself as if your desire is already realised and allow that to be the gateway for you falling asleep and with luck – lucid dreaming your desires.

Card Spread: Healing Path to Wellness, by Kelly-Ann Maddox

This spread is designed to give you encouragement and insight into your healing journey, whether you have been on this path for a while or if you are just beginning.

1. What kinds of resources, tools, or techniques could be good for me right now?

2. Switching to healthier mindsets for my healing journey.

3. Negative influences and unhelpful situations which threaten my healing progress.

4. How to stay safe and on track with my healing journey.

5. Stumbles, setbacks and uncertainty – how to deal?

6. Connecting to 'the why', knowing your intentions and committing anew each day.

Nothing can bring you peace but yourself. – Ralph W. Emerson

Air Journal/Meditation Prompts and Action Points:

~Why do I want to improve my wellness? (Take time with this one; dig a little deeper than what thought first appears.)

~What benefits my mental health right now?

~What destabilises my mental health at the moment?

~What is happening in my internal world at present?

~What is currently occupying my mental capacity?

~What tools, techniques, and resources could be good for me right now?

~What self-sabotaging behaviours am I engaged in?

~What is my most treasured memory?

~A memory that always makes me smile?

~What are some occasions when I have done something that I thought I couldn't do?

~What are the unhelpful mindsets I hold currently?

~One mindset that I want to work on changing first?

~What negative influences are there on me at present that threaten my wellness, and what can I do to lessen their impact on my progress?

~What are the empowering stories that I am telling myself about myself, other people, and the world?

~How can I stay safe on my healing journey?

~How can I handle and cope with any setbacks that arise?

~How do I want to challenge the voice of my inner critic?

~In what ways am I limiting myself through my beliefs about the way things 'have to/should be'?

~What commitment can I make to myself right now?

~What is one key short-term action, implementable immediately, to help me strengthen my connection to inner peace?

~Make a playlist of upbeat songs/music that fills you with energy and happy feelings.

~Create a video playlist of things that make you laugh/ happy. This could be particular scenes from TV shows or films, snippets of jokes from comedians, animal videos, funny fail or win videos, etc., and watch when needed.

~Create a list of things that make you laugh and bring you joy and refer to it when you're feeling a bit low. Have it available on your phone for if you're not at home. You could also make a visual of this list – create an art piece, collage, or picture board of visual representations of these things to serve as a reminder of this list (great for shared spaces or bringing a little of 'you' into a room).

~What activities raise your vibration and get you out of a slump or emotional low? E.g. dancing. List them all out and add to it as you realise more things. Use this list whenever you feel an energy dip and need a boost or to change up your energy a little. This can also be thought of as a safe actions list that you can go to if you feel bad.

When you're in a dark place, you think you've been buried, but actually, you've been planted. – Christine Caine

Fire
Energy flows
where your
intention goes

7: FIRE ~ PART I
AS WITHIN

I take inspired action to make my life the best it can be, following my joy and passion as it leads me to the Truest version of me.

***

Fire is passion, creativity and action. It brings light and warmth, but also burns when out of control, just as we can when we become too consumed with one thing to the detriment of everything else. Fire is considered a fast-paced element and is linked to beta brainwaves that are seen when concentrating. This section aims to raise your confidence further and give you clarity on who your True Self really is. It is about developing your intuition, trust in yourself, and helping you to create meaning in your life and perhaps realise your inner creativity and goals. Fire also deals with the existential and that which makes us very much spiritual beings having a human experience.

Connecting with Fire

Before we dive into the Fire chapter, take some time to connect with the Fire element and journal your responses so you can look over them at a later time. How does Fire interplay with your life? How do you handle heat? Are you happier hot or cool? What types of things ignite your passions? Are you particularly attracted to any of the colours thought to be fiery? What forms of Fire are your favourite and do they play much of a part in your life?

What's your relationship like to the Sun? What about spicy foods? Do you often struggle to feel inspired or is that something that rarely troubles you? How about motivation – would you say you are self-motivated, or do you need a lot of external encouragement or feedback? Do you often feel restless or bored – what about/with? Do you actually take time in your life to pursue passions?

Also, reflect upon whether you have instances of Fire running away with you – are you ever hot-headed or fuming? What causes that for you, and how does it affect life? Do you take inspired action and channel the energy into something productive, or does it wreak a destructive force in your life and mind? Jotting your thoughts to these questions should give you a starting point to understand whether the Fire element plays a strong role in your life currently.

Don't be pushed around by your problems, be led by your dreams.
– Ralph Waldo Emerson

Increasing and Cultivating Motivation

Motivation can seem a little fickle. Many people seem to believe that they either have it or they don't and they must wait for it to appear! It's actually like inspiration, though. People seem more open to the idea of seeking inspiration and cultivating it, so it's more of a continual presence in their lives, but seldom approach motivation in the same way. Yes, it's true that you can wake up suddenly inspired, as if a fairy godmother sprinkled magick dust on you in the night and 'Hey presto!' Inspiration practically is sparking around your head! And you're likely to have experienced the same with motivation – you just *suddenly* feel it!

So, isn't it simple to think you can create motivation too? I think that's great, as I'm not really one for waiting around for things to happen at random. One trick is to actually focus on seeking inspiration or work on lifting your mood because these are gateways that can actually lead to you feeling more motivated or just ready to do the thing!

You can also create easily accessible and available reminders of your *why*. The reasons you want to achieve something or get somewhere should be motivating and inspiring for you, whether or not the action you need to take is a direct means to an end that you *do* want to reach. If not, I would encourage you to ask yourself whether this thing is your desire or someone else's? Do you really care about the outcome or is it just not important to you anymore? Perhaps there is some sort of fear around this thing – fear of change, fear of what it would mean? How does staying the same with this thing fit in with your self-story, your internal narrative about who you are and why you are the way that you are?

If answering those questions, you conclude that you do actually want to do this thing, then how can you make it easier for yourself?

~Are there unnecessary drains on your energy and time that you can alter?

~Does your action plan need revising?

~Do you need to review your vision board or similar thing if you have one?

~Do you need a buddy who is also going through a similar process or struggling with motivation themselves so you can support and encourage each other at the same time? ~Would it be helpful to ask for support from someone else and have them be an ally who can hold you accountable within agreed boundaries?

These thought points should help you to reboot dwindling motivations.

Following on from this, you may realise your motivation is limited because the task at hand seems like a lot of effort or just too big of a commitment. In that case, chunk it down and focus only on taking the first step or just doing it for say, one hour, and repeat positive affirmations and mantras to help get you going, i.e. 'I am committed to making my dreams a reality,' 'My next action will bring me closer to my dreams,' 'I feel good when I do something for my dreams and push myself a little,' 'I don't need for things to be perfect before I begin – the perfect time is now,' 'I know enough to start.' You may like to ask yourself daily this question: '*What can I do today that will progress me further to where I want to be/closer to who I want to be?*'

Sometimes it helps to just do something else and build on from the momentum; however, it still needs to be something productive. A great solution to this is to ask yourself 'What can I do right now to help someone else?' and go do it right away!

In a similar vein, sometimes it's about switching up the energy you find yourself in. Movement is a big helper here because it's the inverse of stagnation and is literally vitality in motion. If your mood's low or you're feeling depressed, which saps motivation more often than not, then this is why dance has been shown to be so beneficial – vitality is the opposite of depression.

If you can just take the few seconds it takes to switch on some of your favourite music and bop around to it for a few minutes, it's quite likely you'll then feel like actually *doing* something – you just have to choose to make that the next action. Other times, you may find a change of scenery is what you need, going outside and getting in nature or someplace bustling with busy people can help you get some perspective, depending on you and what inspires you.

The world does not exist to fill us up, we exist to fill the world up with who we are. – Russell Brand

Putting Perfectionism in its Place

Don't let 'perfect' be the enemy of 'good'. Many people, my past-self included, struggle with perfectionism because it is linked to our self-esteem, especially self-worth. Self-worth is often tied to output, and hence, people with perfectionistic streaks often find it difficult to truly relax – they're always *doing*. Furthermore, when they think they're relaxing, they are guilting themselves for resting and not *doing* or thinking of the apparent million other things that they 'ought' to be doing … What a terrible cycle to be a part of.

This is definitely one of those instances where daily affirmations come in handy so that you can keep reaffirming to yourself that your value is not linked to your output, such as 'I allow myself to have a true balance in my life and that includes making time to relax and fully be present in those moments.' 'I find joy in the moments I do not expect.' 'My value is not in my output – it's in me being my true and most joyous and authentic self.'

In addition, journal through the resistances you feel to this. If you need some prompts to get started, try: When was the last time you let yourself relax without berating yourself for doing so? How was your life at that time, and how was your mental health? What, in detail, is so bad about not being perfect? How do other people around you respond when you're attempting to be perfect? What would happen if you had a balance in your life of the things to be done, having fun, social connection time, and relaxation time?

If you're always doing, you may need to list your priorities and readdress really where you're putting your energy (see energy discovery exercise on page 168).

If you find yourself spending more time cleaning than anything else, know that you're not alone – this is an incredibly common issue. You may find it helpful to sit down with anyone else you live with (or a trusted friend if you live alone) and calmly draw up a list that you can put on the fridge/somewhere easily visible of all of the household tasks and the appropriate amount of time to spend doing them and how frequently, e.g. vacuum every other day for twenty minutes, clean floors once a week for thirty minutes. What's appropriate for your home will not necessarily be the same as anyone else's. This is a way of drawing up a boundary around this area though for your wellbeing, and let's face it, sanity!

It also helps greatly to assess the perspective you look at evidence of a lived-in space with, in other words, general mess. For example, cooking splashes can be evidence of a lovingly prepared nutritious and yummy meal if you choose to see them that way. It's already slightly less annoying viewing it this way, and then you can respectfully use I statements and help people do things differently, so it creates less clean-up in the first place (see Water section).

Apply this method to anything else you feel it would help with.

Ask yourself often throughout the day: Is this a priority right now/do I *have* to do this now? And get comfortable with the temporary discomfort that comes from doing something else instead.

Mindfulness would be particularly helpful here too, so study and practice that and learn to notice the perfectionism when it stirs and gently remind it that it isn't necessary and let it go in favour of another way of being. Get comfortable with the discomfort that comes from not being perfect – take your time, it won't happen overnight. Breaking the perfection cycle can be tricky, but it is doable, and know that peace is on the opposite side of perfectionism.

Feel Congruent - Understand Your Values

Our values are beliefs that we hold close to our heart. They are foundational as they shape our identity and inform how we operate within the world and how we feel about things that are done or said. When we understand what our values are, we are able to live with more clarity, and that is beneficial to general wellness because we can recognise unhappiness that comes from a value not being realised or being in conflict with someone else's.

We can clash with people who have opposing values, and it's really useful to consider complementary values in those who we may choose to live with and be in long-term relationships with, especially romantic and business. Entering into partnerships with people whom we are ultimately going to be on different pages with only leads to frustration, disappointment, sadness, anguish, and sometimes loathing, as I have seen time and time again through my counselling work. When we understand how our values influence us, it makes it easier to live and make decisions with more congruence as you can more easily navigate conflicts and choices that arise in your life, particularly those that relate to other people.

Phrases such as 'pushing my buttons' relate back to personal values and the feeling we get when someone else is not acting in accordance with a value that we hold. Having our buttons pushed is an opportunity to perform Shadow Work though (see the Spirit section for more on Shadow Work), and in particular, it can inform us of a value that we have that is being disrespected. For example, if you felt somewhat frustrated that someone had not stuck to their word on something, you value integrity and perhaps have a strong principle of personal honour.

This in turn can help with emotional management and mental wellness because you are better able to see what exactly it was about the interaction or situation that rattled you, which means that you're in a more advantageous position to navigate that situation and make it more likely that the value be met next time, whether that would be through clearer communication or from setting boundaries or choosing more carefully whom to trust.

Through this self-awareness, you're also less likely to ruminate on situations trying to figure out why you feel so crappy from them – you get straight to the point and have no need to dwell or prolong hurtful emotions. I advocate the need to understand our values a lot because I see the impacts of a lack of clarity in this area. Values can be thought of as symbols around a compass, rather like the alethiometer in Phillip Pullman's *His Dark Materials* book series. Your personal compass will feel right when the needles are pointing to the values that matter most to you – in other words, you will feel congruent and in alignment with yourself. The following exercise can help you value self-awareness.

In between goals is a thing called life, that has to be lived and enjoyed. – Sid Caesar

Get Aligned – Value Discovery Exercise

Choose from the words below those that are important to you by writing them out, adding any words that you'd like. Then circle the ten that you feel most strongly about and rank them from 1-10, with 1 as most important: achievement, adventure, autonomy, balance, beauty, calmness, connection, creativity, fairness, family, freedom, friendship, fun, honesty, humour, independence, integrity, knowledge, love, loyalty, morals, nature, openness, peace, popularity, power, recognition, relaxation, respect, responsibility, safety, self-reliance, simplicity, spirituality, stability, success, time, trust, variety, wealth, wisdom.

Next, look at where in your life (the life area) your need for that value to be realised is met, such as through community, family, fitness, friendship, health, leisure, parenting, religion, romantic partnership, work, etc., and write that next to the value.

For each of the life areas you've written, take time to write your answers to these four questions for them:

1. How do I feel in this life area at the moment?
2. What is currently going well in this area/what I am happy with here?
3. What would my life ideally look and feel like in this area?
4. What do I need to do to bring me closer to my ideal in this area?

After doing this exercise, you should find that you're at a better place to see the big picture of your life now and operate from alignment with your values, which is part of being congruent and a more authentic version of yourself.

This exercise can be performed annually or whenever you feel that you would like to check in with yourself, because sometimes values change, or we develop new ones.

Authenticity is the daily practice of letting go of who we think we're supposed to be and embracing who we are. – Brené Brown

Embrace Authenticity

The etymology of the word authenticity is 'author', so 'being authentic' is you writing your own story and narrative. Living in accordance with my values has helped lessen anxiety, and others I know who've turned their focus to this feel the benefits too. They feel much more grounded. Being involved in things bigger than yourself can help by allowing your own life to be a bit more in perspective – things that give you a sense of community or global connection, and usually something that benefits others. This could be volunteering or activism of some kind. As you embrace your uniqueness more, you are clearer about your desires which gives you a sense of direction. Having a sense of direction is calming in itself because it can narrow the point of focus and give you comfort from the sense that you're heading towards something great and making some difference.

Another way to discover more of your authentic self is to tap into your childhood self – the version of you when you were much less influenced by other people's opinions and agendas and you were perhaps more in tune with your intuition and emotions. A way to tap into this version of yourself for inspiration is to get nostalgic. Think back to all of the things that you remember about your childhood – what were the things that captured your imagination then, sparked your curiosity, creativity, and you just loved?

Besides listing these things and journaling what comes up for you about them and how it applies to you now, a great way to get into your childhood mind can be to watch a favourite film from back then, look through photographs, or reread a favourite childhood book. It can be surprising how things can alter in magickal ways when you review them as an adult. This is about rediscovering the joys of your younger self and seeing whether there is anything in those for you now and whether you want to follow that thread to see where it can lead your current self.

A Concept That Can Spark an Idea – Nomenclature

I'd always known what my names meant in terms of etymology, as I had framed little cards detailing facts about my names in my room growing up. I suppose my interest stemmed from there originally, so I had a private curiosity in nomenclature as a concept moving forwards.

You could think of it in a similar fashion as some people are interested in star signs and the influence they do or don't have upon people. I came across a research study that tracked people with different types of names, and it was interested in whether that had any bearing on how satisfied they were in their life and what they did as a career or job. Another study suggested there was a bearing on people's names and what they went on to do with their life, part of a self-fulfilling prophecy.

Now I don't want to make anyone concerned about their name. Remember that a rose by any other name would still smell as sweet. I just couldn't help being curious about this concept, and at a time when I was struggling to know who I was and what on Earth I was doing here, it was a little light in the distance – a starting point to explore. So I did, and I liked where it led, and I have consciously allowed this to be a slight guiding principle in my life moving forwards. It's influenced some decisions and even the name of my business: Sophie Wild Robin, which is a play on my birth names.

Understanding more about the etymological history of my name also helped me to accept it because, for a large time in growing up, I rejected my name. I did not write my 'real' name and experimented with different ones, trying them on as you might a pair of shoes before you decide if they're 'you' enough (my parents would laugh at the mail that would get addressed to these 'other people' who lived with them! Don't worry, it was nothing of a legal nature, mostly junk mail and website sign-ups when you don't need card details). I didn't believe my name 'fitted' me. While that may seem trivial in the grand scheme of things, it was a manifestation of a crisis of Self and highlighted that there was work to do on myself. I love my name now and wouldn't change it. So, explore your name history if you feel curious to – it may lead you to fun and magickal places!

On a similar note, if you are stuck with issues around 'identity' and 'purpose', there are so many avenues spiritual people may like to explore depending on their beliefs to see if they do spark any inspiration, such as numerology, astrology, past lives, the Celtic Ogham and even the much-loved Myers-Briggs test.

Working with Archetypes to Uncover Your Identity

Archetypes are a hugely helpful concept to help you discover more about yourself, who you were, who you are now, and who you'd like to be a bit more like. They are useful because they transcend culture, religion, and gender, and there is so much choice, the possibilities are practically endless! You can draw archetypes from tarot, pop culture, comic series, video games, novels, film and TV, historical figures, deities, or devise your own.

It would be beneficial to use your journal for this as it's often something that isn't done all in one go and it can be used as a reference tool in the future. Firstly, it can be helpful to think what archetypes you're drawn to in particular and jot these down. If you're struggling a little to think of archetypes, then you may like to write a list of eight or so people whom you admire (alive or deceased) instead.

If you're really, really stuck and new to this, then Carolyn Myss has cards and other resources inspired by the work of Carl Jung (an early pioneer of the shadow unconscious) on this subject, which can be a great jumping-off point.

To use generic archetypes as an example for myself when I did this exercise a few years ago, I identified five main archetypes for me at the time: the hippy, the rebel, the creative, the mystic, and the student. Once you have your main archetypes, it's a good idea to write them each on separate pieces of paper and draw/collage them. Around the name/picture, write the characteristics of each – that which identifies them. You could even include their common thoughts, company they keep, phrases, style, habitats, type of voice, energy level, habits, postures, colours, elements they're in tune with, objects they use, symbols, their main message, preferences and dislikes.

Once you feel you have explored the archetype as an individual and have a clear sense of who each one is and how they operate within the world, ask yourself and write:

~Why you are drawn to that person/archetype?

~What it is about these archetypes/people you admire?

~What do you not like so much or is uncomfortable about the archetype for you (this can be its shadow side)?

~What do you identify within the archetype that was present with a past version of yourself and what does that mean for you now that it's not as much in your present?

~Is there anything within the archetypes that you want to be a part of your future Self, and how can you make it so?

This exercise can be performed annually if you like as a check-in or if you happen to feel a little lost with who you are. Particularly with the archetypes you wish to embrace more in your future, you can choose to work with these as you might a deity or animal totem to help you embrace them more now and allow them to play an active role in your life or serve simply as a daily inspiration source.

If archetypes are a little too abstract or vast for you at the moment, another way of performing this exercise is to take five people that you admire and list out exactly what it is that you admire about them and why. Once you've done this, have a look whether you can categorise anything that you've written. Have you written characteristics about their personality, appearance, skills, life or other? The amount you have placed in each category may indicate to you what your focus is on right now.

Take a few moments to assess your feelings about that – is it what you expected? Are you happy about it? What do the categories that you have written less in tell you? Are they the aspects that you're satisfied with in your own life, or are they things you're avoiding?

The idea with archetypes is to give you a focus and a potential mirror for yourself with which to examine what is going on for you. Any archetype can be illuminating for you if you apply it to yourself and see what thoughts and feelings come up. Keep digging and uncovering the layers – see what secrets your unconscious is hiding!

Deepening Self-awareness – Morning Pages

This is a journaling technique created by Julia Cameron that can be used in the long-term, and a habit can be created around this as part of a morning routine. It is stream-of-consciousness writing where you put pen to paper or fingers to keyboard and allow your thoughts to simply flow through onto the page. This typically takes three pages of writing but at least one side of A4.

You will soon discover the state of your mind that day, and it often presents you with obvious action steps that you can take throughout the day to feel better or be more aligned with what you want. Those who do this regularly often find that it helps with their creativity, and it can be a wonderful way to get things off your chest before you start the day. It's done in the morning, soon after waking because this is when we are usually our most unfiltered and genuine self. Journaling in general is a helpful way to reflect and gain clarity but note that awareness doesn't necessarily equal acceptance.

Choose a Power Word

You may choose an empowering word or concept to be your focus of the month, year, or another time period. In the past, I have chosen the word *queen,* which is also an archetype, as well as *calm, love, compassion, intention, joy, focus, success.* The word can be anything you like.

The idea is to really take the time to explore the word as a concept, which means figuring out what it means to you, how it operates within and affects your life, whether you have any shadows, resistances or blocks to it, and how you want it to inform the choices and decisions that you make while it's your power word.

You are essentially getting to know and understand the word and its meaning on a deep and personal level, learn from it as it teaches you. The word then becomes empowering to you and can be a useful compass point, something that helps you navigate your life in a positive manner because without being clear on our inner compass, we risk seeking outside of ourselves for the things that are only found within ...

When *love* was my power word for the year, I looked at everything I could through that word as if it was a filter. I asked myself whether what I said, wrote, and decided was in the alignment of love. I had to balance self-love with love for others, and it helped me to make wiser choices moving forwards.

So, pick a word and allow it to be your teacher and guide for a while and see what you learn from it. It can help you reshape how you navigate your life.

Courage is a love affair with the unknown. – Osho

Create a Personal Power Sigil

Sigils are a symbolic representation of your intention or desired outcome for a spell. They are similar to symbols but tend to be formed with a combination of symbols, including letters, numbers and 'made-up' symbols created by their designer. Bind-runes are a common form of sigil magick where a few runes are combined together in a meaningful way to the practitioner.

Sigils can involve taking symbols and drawing them backwards, upside-down, or on an angle, having some be larger or smaller than others, and be in different colours. Whatever lends itself best to the intention of the designer, and so, they are a simple and useful form of magick that can be used on their own or as part of any spells and rituals.

For this particular sigil, create one that reminds you of your purpose or perhaps you'd find it more useful to have one that reminds you of who you *are.* You can create one for anything! A goal, an emotion, an intention.

Use them to add extra oomph in spells and rituals, draw them into your food and stir into your drink, write on your body with lotion before you rub it in, draw it on yourself with henna in a ritual to empower the symbol (and you), draw it with glue before you paste something into your grimoire, journal, or scrapbook, paint it before you create something on your canvas, embroider it onto a garment or accessory, draw it on your notebooks and bookmarks, draw on yourself with a special oil before a ritual or important occasion, draw it on the back of photographs … the possibilities are many!

When I was first working on trying to change my mindset and be free of unhelpful and hurtful thoughts, I drew my personal sigil in glitter glue several times on paper and stuck them around my room and on my things. The addition of glitter meant it was more eye-catching and thus harder to overlook, so the symbol registered more often in my conscious and unconscious mind – deepening its positive effect. Nowadays I draw sigils in pretty metallic and shimmery felts which catch the light and my eye.

If you don't want to go around drawing 'strange symbols' everywhere then fret not – there's a strong school of thought that with sigils, they gain power when they're unseen (occulted). This is because of the *as above, so below, as within, so without.* Some of the most powerful things in our world are unseen, such as air, light waves, gravity, and those pesky beliefs and fears you aren't aware you're operating from yet. We can detect them, yes, but see them as clearly as we see our hand we cannot, but they are no less powerful because of it.

Too many of us are not living our dreams because we are living our fears. – Lee Brown

FIRE ~ PART II
SO WITHOUT

Don't dance around the perimeter of who you want to be, dive in fully and completely. – Gabrielle Bernstein

***

Fire Meditation

Meditation is a way to rest in existence and be consciously aware of your experience and intuition. You can technically meditate anywhere. It works great when your mind is starting to become calmer as you regain control over your thoughts, and your mind is becoming more of a space where you are your own best friend. It can help a lot with wellness when your mind is at the place where it is more accepting of more helpful thoughts or just feels a little lighter, if not straight away before you do any conscious work on your mind. Some people will have success with meditation before that point, but if that's not your experience, then you're not alone – it's common to struggle initially. Simply work through other exercises that allow you to regain control over your thoughts and return to meditation later. Just because it's not for you right now, doesn't mean it won't be in future. You can build up from as little as one minute a day – start as small as you need to, it's better than not starting at all.

It can help to have a focus for meditation and sometimes it's nice to do anyway to mix it up a little. Either at your sacred space or somewhere else that you can make comfortable, light a candle in front of you and sit and centre yourself.

Once you feel that you have stilled, gaze at the flame. You don't need to stare at it, let your focus soften. Witness the flame, see all of its shades and movements.

Gaze for as long as desired. If your attention wanders, simply return it back to the flame.

This simple act has all of the wonderful benefits of meditation but is a lot easier for many people than having their eyes closed and focusing on the breath. The same can be done with running water, such as with a fountain or raindrops on a window, incense smoke, and trees or clouds on a breezy day.

Don't move the way fear makes you move. Move the way love make your move. Move the way joy makes you move. – Osho

Discover Where Your Energy is Going – an Exercise

This exercise helps you discover where you need to find more balance in your life. Balance doesn't necessarily mean that everything is equal in terms of time, money, effort and energy, it's more that it *feels* equally good in each area.

To complete this exercise, take some scrap paper and write each area of your life down – whatever is important to you, it's totally personal. For me, it is home, work, business, travel/experiences, husband, family, friends, health and fitness, mind, spirituality, and creativity. Rip or cut each area out so you have 'labels' with each area on.

Next, go and get as many receptacles of roughly equal capacity, e.g. similarly sized glasses (clear or transparent works best) as you have areas, line them up in front of you and assign each a label. Fill a jug or bottle, as big as you can find, with cold water and perhaps a little food colouring or cordial to make it easier to see.

Consider the area where you spend the least amount of energy and pour a little water in its corresponding vessel, or if you currently spend no energy there, leave it empty. Work your way up until you have where you spend your most amount of energy with the most amount of water in its corresponding glass.

Note your results down or draw into your journal; you can even photograph this for future reference.

Next, assess what you have in front of you: are you happy with what you see – do you like how your energy is distributed between each area? What would you alter – where would you like to spend less/more energy?

Tip all of the water back into the original jug and redistribute it – this time to reflect your ideal energy distribution. Note this outcome down and photograph.

How can you create the balance that you desire: how could you spend less energy in the areas you don't want to spend as much in? How can you cultivate time for more energy in the areas you want more time and energy in? What actions or disciplines may need to be put in place to realise this change? What conversations need to be had or what boundaries need to be exercised, and with whom? How much motivation do you have to make this version your reality? How can you ride high motivation or increase low motivation?

Create a Signature Scent for Personal Power

Blending different oils was one of my favourite things to do when I first got into witchcraft, because I found scent to be such a powerful mood-changer. Many people can attest to having experienced a certain smell bringing up a long unrecalled memory or being thrown into an instant nostalgia. I love mixing and matching scents to a space or purpose. Not only is this a pretty fun process but it has a meditative quality, as blending scents requires you to focus fully into the present and tune in to how each scent makes you feel and then combine them appropriately. It's such an easy way to bring more magick and intention into a moment!

As previously mentioned, you can dress candles with oils or simply pop them into an oil burner or diffuser, add them to dried herb pouches to gently scent your drawers and wardrobe or in open bowls like potpourri. With the abundance of scented candles and diffusers nowadays, blending your own is a subtle way to weave magick without raising suspicion if that is a concern for you.

Learning the traditional magickal properties of flora can be a great place to start – you just need to check in with yourself to see if you agree with the property, as you may feel very differently about it. I have taken a lot of time to blend my own oils for different purposes. I have oils I use specifically when meditating, for specific types of spells and rituals, and for particular moods I want to enhance or create, such as peace and safety at night-time. The same would apply if you were blending your own dried herbs and resins for incenses or consumption-safe flora for teas.

One thing that is certainly fun is to create your own signature scent. This is a blend that communicates to the world through scent who you are and what you're about. It would be a wonderful thing to do your research and gather everything you need ready to create the scent in sacred space during a ritual.

This is a great declaration of self-love and personal power, and is a great thing you can do on your birthday as a really lovely gift to yourself. You will need to research skin-safe varieties of oils and about carriers (which make blends safe for skin contact) and take extra precaution as certain flora counteract medications and are not safe for use when pregnant. There are a few book recommendations in the resource section if you want to learn for yourself. If you're stuck with where to start, consider the type of smells you're drawn to and try to analyse why or what they mean to you and how you feel when smelling them.

If you're not performing this on your birthday, simply pick the Moon phase and weekday you feel most powerful in (if you want to be extra, you can choose the time of day or work with numerology as well) or perform on the full Moon or midday Sun, if that's more you (we're not all Moon babies, and that's okay). Astrology people may like to pick the Moon phase and day/time they were born on if that's possible. Spellcraft can be as symbol-heavy as you like, but it isn't necessary; your clear will and intent is always the most important part of any magick.

Take time to calm and centre yourself to prepare psychologically for the ritual. Cast your circle and do anything else you feel appropriate, such as playing certain music. I have playlists for everything, and of course I have a personal power playlist of music that makes me feel aligned to myself and really capable and stable.

When your intent is clear, begin to blend the oils while thinking of and chanting the values that they represent, and the messages they give to the outside world about you.

Once you're happy with your blend, anoint yourself with the oil on your third eye, throat, wrists and feet and commit to expressing your authentic Self.

Decorate the bottle containing your blend however you wish and draw your personal power sigil onto it. You can even name and label the blend your power word if that feels right to you.

Close the circle and wear your *you* scent whenever you need reminding to stay aligned to who you are, or you want to give yourself a boost.

Full-Waning Moon, Fire Releasing Ritual

This ritual utilises the power of the full-waning Moon (the time when the Moon appears full but has actually entered into its waning transition) to release that which no longer serves you. There are apps and websites that can use your geolocation to tell you the precise time the Moon will change its phase if you need assistance to work it out.

For this ritual you may like to use whichever of the following symbolise releasing for you: a candle (white or black would work for me), incense/herb bundle, paper, pen, crystal, a lighter/matchbox, and a cauldron or other fire-safe bowl, dish, or bin.

Cast a circle and burn the incense/herb bundle to cleanse yourself and your space – willing the cleanse as you do. Sit and meditate holding the crystal and visualise whatever it is you want to release, leaving you and your life. When you're ready, write on the paper 'I release …' and list everything you're letting go of '… from my life.'

When you've finished writing, open your circle, take the cauldron and paper and look at the Moon, preferably outside if you're able. Take the paper and carefully light it and drop it into the cauldron. As it burns, chant 'I release you' nine times (the number commonly associated with completion). When it's ash, you may dispose of the ash as you see fit and return to your circle to close it and ground yourself. You should now feel more able to focus on what is important and confidently move forwards.

* * *

Sometimes, it doesn't feel quite right to release something with Fire. Fire is quite dramatic and fast-acting in terms of energy exchange – it converts its host medium (the combustible) and oxygen rapidly into flame. If this is ever the case for you, there are other ways to release. You can tailor the above ritual to suit your needs and work in a way that reflects the element that you feel more called to work with at the moment, or for this particular thing you're releasing.

Earth is considered the slowest acting of the elements with regards to bringing about change, and is thought to be for time spans of months to a year; so if that feels right, bury your paper whole or ripped up instead.

Water is considered medium-paced, depending on the form you use, and is thought to span times of a few weeks to a month (similar to the lunar cycle). You can gather fallen leaves (preferably from your garden or as close to you as possible to symbolise that it is something *you* are letting go that was once in your life/space) that would allow you to write on them with chalk or a marker. Write on the leaves instead of the paper what you want to let go and release them into a stream or river. Another way is to write on paper with a water-soluble ink or pencil and wash it gently under a tap. As the water flows over it and displaces the writing, perform the visualisations as described in the ritual. In the past, I've written things in chalk outside and let the rain wash them away.

Air is considered to act with a pace that isn't as fast as Fire but isn't as slow as Water, so we're looking at a couple of weeks to several days. A way to work with Air is to also gather fallen leaves and write on them but release instead into the wind as it blows on a blustery day.

These are but a few examples of what you can do. Allow yourself to get creative and inspired with how you choose to tailor rituals to best meet your intentions and needs – that's how you perform the most powerful magick – it reflects *you!* I hope that this also demonstrates that you don't necessarily have to perform rituals and elaborate spells or have many fancy props. Witchcraft nurtures your creativity because if you want to do something with intent, you need only use what you have around you. Every moment can be a little magickal if you will it so and put that extra thought and action in. Witchcraft builds your resourcefulness and imagination for the possibilities, which happens to be a wonderful boon to wellness!

FEAR mantra = face everything and rise. – Marie Forleo

Courage, Confidence, and Success Ritual

This is a simple ritual to do when you'd benefit from a little extra boost in your confidence, particularly before doing something that you are nervous about. A ritual like this, is usually performed during the midday Sun as it is at its peak, as the Sun represents confidence and shining strong, but do it at whatever time of day/night for you most resonates with the theme.

For spell components, consider which of the following represent courage to you: incense (I like a spicy and citrusy blend such as cinnamon and orange), a candle (dressed if you like), and a crystal and/or the strength card of the tarot major arcana (you can print one you like if you don't have a deck with this card); you'll also need a pen and a couple of sheets of paper.

You may also wish to create a playlist for this spell of a few songs or music pieces that make you feel supercharged with confidence when you hear them.

Cleanse the space and yourself and cast a circle if you like. Play the music and light the candle. Centre yourself and hold your chosen crystal and/or strength card.

Focus upon the feeling of courage and confidence and allow it to fill you. If you are struggling with this, take the paper and write your strengths and the accomplishments that you are proud of, and you can also think of instances when other people have seemed confident to you. To onlookers, confident people often seem brave and courageous in the moment they are shining.

Next, allow your mind to turn towards the things that are coming up that you want to feel confident in doing and go through them, seeing yourself being and feeling totally confident in each. Trusting yourself and your abilities.

Write 'I am' affirmations for these ('I am confident with …' 'I have courage with …' 'I trust in my abilities to handle …' 'I am doing … with perfect ease', etc.).

When you are ready, fold the paper in half twice in a towards-you motion, repeating your affirmations aloud as you do. Place it on your altar or somewhere visible and safe with the crystal and/or strength card on top, and close the circle.

After completing this ritual, take five minutes to journal anything that stands out to you as something you may need to take action on, such as with a public speaking task; perhaps you can also increase your confidence by rehearsing speaking in front of a mirror and then with loved ones.

By taking inspired action like this, you're showing that you care and are willing to do what's necessary to ensure your confidence and success grows, with the added boost of having a spell behind you. To use a video-game/fantasy analogy, think of it as enchanting your armour or weapons to enhance their effectiveness.

You can then review this list whenever necessary, or daily if you need to, and carry the crystal/card as a token to remind you of the confidence you felt during this ritual.

Card Spread: Hidden Treasure, by Kelly-Ann Maddox

Use this spread for whenever you feel that you have lost touch with your abilities, skills and strengths, or for if you have no idea and are curious about what the cards you choose may reveal to you. Perhaps you have been suppressing a hidden treasure! This spread will help you to access it, embrace it, and celebrate what you find!

1. Hidden treasure – my secret strengths and superpowers.

2. Possible reasons why this treasure remains hidden.

3. How to bring my treasure out of hiding for the world!

4. Potential trouble to be wary of when rocking my hidden treasure.

5. Potential positive results from owning and using my hidden treasure.

6. Why now's a great time to wear my treasure with pride.

The cave you fear to enter holds the treasure you seek.
– Joseph Cambell

We are all multi-faceted, more like disco balls than ping-pong balls! We have different dimensions to our personalities, interests, histories, and different 'hats' that we wear throughout our days sometimes, depending on who we are with and what we are doing. This makes us interesting, and it's okay if you're not everyone's cup of tea – not everyone is yours either, so don't make the mistake of trying to be everything for everyone because you'll water yourself down and extinguish your unique spark!

Fire Journal/Meditation Prompts and Action Points:

~What Fire-related issue do I want to work on right now?

~What is the hardest part of my life at present?

~What's the hardest thing to let go of right now?

~What builds my confidence?

~What gives me hope and agency within the world?

~What has influenced me to be who I am now?

~What do I activate in others?

~Do I feel creatively burnt out? – If so, what fun new skill could I learn or try (i.e. coding, crystallomancy, knitting, needle felting, palmistry, pyrography, rollerblading, sculpting, smithing, tasseography, weaving) to reignite my spark?

~What are my deepest desires?

~With whom do I feel the most inauthentic, and can I see why?

~In what situations do I feel inauthentic, and why?

~What sparks a sense of childlike curiosity and wonder for me?

~Do I make empowered daily decisions that align with my true self and desires? – If not, how can I?

~What do I currently do that does not resonate with me anymore? (Wrong turns are ok; they simply focus the path.)

~What do I want my life to feel like?

~What are my top ten strengths?

~What traits can I use to my advantage with my goals?

~If I could wake up tomorrow having gained one quality and one ability what would they be?

~What gives me pride about who I am?

~How can I develop my personal power/gift further?

~What does success mean for me – and what's it look and feel like to me? (Define it with clarity.)

~What's something I do every day that makes me happy?

~If I had more 'free time' what would I do more of?

~How will my happiness impact the wider world?

~In what ways is my 'daily' life disconnected from my true passions - and can I alter this for my highest good?

~If a miracle happened overnight while I slept and my life was suddenly as I want it to be, when I wake in the morning, what is the first thing I notice that tells me my life has changed?

~What is one key short-term action, implementable immediately, to help me strengthen my connection to joy/the joyful path?

~What blocks are there to me discovering more of who I am?

~What is stopping me from being who I truly am?

~How can I stay consistently inspired and motivated?

~List the things I would do if I were brave enough.

~List the things I didn't think I would ever do.

~List the challenges that I am now ready to face.

~Make an inspiration list: the sources you can go to for inspiration, including places, people and specific resources.

Courage is resistance to *fear, mastery* of *fear – not absence of fear.*
– Mark Twain

Spirit

You are a Spirit
having a
human experience

8: SPIRIT ~ PART I
AS ABOVE, SO BELOW

I fill my own cup up first, and pour from the overflow.

***

Spirit is you and the bigger picture, and creating balance. It is looking into the long-term of your future and where to go once you have earnestly worked through each of the four elements. It is also your whole Self – your entire being, and can involve your inner child, shadow self, and past lives. Spirit is your connection to others and all things. It's related to gamma brainwaves which are associated with expanded consciousness and insight.

Connecting with Spirit

Take some time now to become still and reflect on your relationship to Spirit, and journal your responses as they come up so that you have a record to reflect back over.

~What does the Spirit element mean to you – can you put your feelings about it into words?

~Do your thoughts ever wander to the bigger picture beyond your life, beyond your part of the world?

~Whatever your response, why do you think that is?

~Do you ever participate in things for the good of your community or the world in some way – what does it mean to you to do so?

~How are you with meditation – has it always come easily to you, or are you needing to exercise a lot of willpower to practice? How do you feel after meditation? Do you feel more connected to yourself, humanity, the planet, the Cosmos, divinity? How has your relationship with these things changed over your life? What further developments would you like in this area? Are you able to tune into yourself and your intuition easily?

All we have to decide is what to do with the time that is given us.
– J. R. R. Tolkien

Long-term Wellness – Self-Care

You can't pour from an empty cup, and when you're burnt out, you're no good to yourself or anyone else. Self-care is the daily practice of refilling your teapot. You know it's drained when you find yourself with little patience, snapping at people, getting annoyed more easily, struggling to concentrate, or sometimes through physical symptoms such as headaches. You need to take care of your mind and body – keep hydrated, move your body regularly, eat when you need to, delegate, say no, assert boundaries, and so on. Self-care is the practice of self-love, and it is you taking responsibility for your life and wellness and preventing burnout. It is as much about intentional relaxation as it is about having fun and requires that you check in with yourself often and give yourself what it is you need.

Consider planning a vacation. This is an annual aim for many people but rather than seeing it as a 'break' from your daily life, see it as the chance to treat yourself to experiencing something/somewhere new, or if you want to return to a place, then see it as a gift to yourself to be somewhere that presents a different kind of fun than what you ordinarily have available. This subtle shift might not seem like much, but in the long-term, how we frame things can go on to have a huge impact on how we feel. Travel is good for the soul and mind, and it gets you out of your normal routine and can give a different perspective to your life as you are literally distant from certain parts of it, so do make sure to consider it as part of self-care.

Daily self-care can look as simple as you preparing a nutritious lunch for yourself for the next day, or planning your outfit the night before so it doesn't take time away from the precious minutes in the morning before a busy day. Self-care is really anything that would look and feel like you *caring* for yourself. Plan daily small things that don't take up too much time, and look forward to the more special things that feel like a treat and are bigger events. Having fun things to look forward to is ridiculously good for our wellness.

To follow with the teapot analogy from earlier, consider each energy type: physical, emotional, mental, and spiritual. Plan one thing each day that restores some energy in each area. When that becomes easy to manage, add in as many activities as you need to, to feel that your teapot is 100% full of each type of energy every day. This doesn't have to look like doing eight self-care activities every day. It will depend on which energy you've been using a lot of or will be using a lot of the next day. For example, an introvert or empath may be aware of a demanding social activity the next day, and they may wish to spend as much time as possible the day before doing things that fill their emotional and mental energy to help tomorrow go smoothly as much as possible.

Just as if you were going for a long and strenuous hike, you would spend the day before gently stretching, resting and eating especially well as you'd be expending physical energy and mental energy to keep going and reach the end of the hike in good time.

Note that restorative activities tend to give more than they take and what activities are truly restorative for you may not be the same for everyone else. Some may be brushing your hair, drinking mindfully, or reading a book – they're some of my favourite restorative activities. If you aren't sure what activities fill which energies, then keep a log of the activity and how you feel after it. The words you use to describe how you feel afterwards should indicate to you which energy you have replenished. For example, if I felt refreshed after a ten-minute meditation to music, I would conclude that for me, that type of meditation allows me to fill up some of my mental energy. If I felt calm after brushing my hair or stroking my cats for a few minutes, I would deduce that for me, those activities restored some of my emotional energy. Keeping a log in this way can really help clarify for you how activities affect you and help you choose activities more wisely in future to match your needs.

This is all planning for long-term self-care because if you are caring for yourself, you're not letting your teapot's brew become weak, sour, stale or empty – you're not going to burn out, and therefore you always have enough energy for yourself and to be able to give to others.

The people who are crazy enough to think they can change the world are the ones who do. – Steve Jobs

Morning Focus – Intention-setting for the Day

We've talked about the importance of a good night-time routine for setting you up to have the best day possible, and the purpose of a morning routine is to set your focus for the day ahead, and many find having that sense of direction to be helpful. You may already know where you want your focus to be: productive, creative, about connection, relaxation, study, environment, etc. If you do not know, then you may wish to be guided. There are a few ways of doing so:

~ You may clear your mind and openly meditate to allow whatever messages that are meant for you to come.

~ Pull an oracle, tarot card, rune, or ogham for the day.

~ Pick a book or dictionary, close your eyes and turn to a chance page, then point to a random place on that page. Whatever word or sentence you land on is your reflection for the day.

I say each morning, *'Where would you have me go, what would you have me do, what would you have me say and to whom.'* This allows me to move past any ego/my own agenda and simply be a conduit for what is right for my clients and those who I meet that day. That is then my intention, whether I have client work or not. I then may set a further focus on top of that as well as remembering my power word of the year or an archetype I am working with. It's also nice to select a crystal that matches my intent for that day and carry it with me or wear jewellery with that crystal in. I often dress in a colour that reflects my intent for the day (see preparation chapter for colour information).

You don't need to do all that to begin with though! Choose one thing that calls to you the most, and you can always build upon it. Never become overwhelmed by feeling you must do all of the things all at once. You will soon burn out and need to start again. One small alteration or addition at a time is how to make lasting progress.

Forever is composed of nows. – Emily Dickinson

Gradually Increase Your Baseline Mood – Gratitude

A simple way to increase baseline mood is to add more gratitude into your life. This could be something you list before bed – making it specific to that day – or as part of a morning routine to help set you up for the day ahead (or do both). Either way, it's difficult to let things get so on top of you or focus on what you don't have when you realise you have a lot of blessings, even if it is simply safe drinking water and that you are able to read this book.

Look at your life and what brings you happiness. Keep a separate journal for gratitude and daily write at least three things you're truly thankful for. Really feel it as you write and put *why* you are grateful for it too. The why is important as it is what actually allows you to feel the gratitude. Being grateful for what you presently have is a huge part of successful spellcasting where you are asking for something new or different. Also, this can be helpful for deepening your self-awareness as over time. You can discover more about your values from your whys, which only helps with living more authentically, congruently, and within your personal vibration.

You could also do this with whomever you live with in the evening, each sharing something that day you're particularly thankful for and why. It's a great way to get children involved or adults who are more reluctant to share in positive experiences. If you live on your own, perhaps call someone and do this in the evening.

What is useful about writing something down daily is that if there is a time when you are feeling very low and struggling, you can look back through the book and remind yourself of these blessings you have or have experienced. This can alter your perspective and 'reset' your thinking back to a way which serves and is helpful to you again. If you struggle with going beyond the basics with gratitude, ask yourself: What do I need to do more of that actually brings me joy, peace, and comfort? How can I fit in more of what fills me up in my life?

Whenever you feel your mood drop or yourself getting into 'shoulds, coulds and woulds' or getting into anxiety, switch your thinking by turning to gratitude. Allow yourself to really feel into all of the people, pets, and things you love. Go through the elements if you like and think of all the things you love which fall into each of them. Let your joy for having those things present in your life warm you from the inside.

It's not joy that makes us grateful; it is gratitude that makes us joyful.
– Brother David Steindl-Rast

Charging a Piece of Jewellery or an Accessory

There are many beautiful ways to charge something, and this act can take a mundane object and make it a little more magickal and purposeful. Charging is similar to consecrating except that with charging, you may only be using one specific element (or none) with which to imbue your object with a specific power or quality. You can charge a previously consecrated object; in fact, you may believe that to enhance the power of the object further.

So, consider what power you may charge something with. It could be love, so that when you connect with the item, you are reminded of all of the love present in your life. This can be useful, for example, when you are feeling slightly alone and full of self-doubt, helping you shift your vibration and thoughts back towards something more fruitful and positive for you. You may charge the jewellery with power itself, so that you are filled with confidence and self-trust before an important event or when you're working on challenging a fear. As always, the possibilities are only as limited as your imagination!

It is common to charge an item of jewellery because they often lend themselves to being worm with intention, so charging them makes sense and only adds to their significance. However, you may charge a specific object, say, an ornament on your desk so that each time you lose focus, you hold the object and can more easily ground yourself back into your task.

How you charge something depends on the item and the power you want to charge it with. What things in the natural world remind you of the feeling you want the object to hold, and what elements match the vibration of the feeling or power too? For example, you may wish to charge a silver ring with peace (because silver is associated with the Moon and that is considered more peaceful than the vibrant energy of the Sun and gold which are its opposites), so that when you wear it and touch it, you feel more at peace and can more easily let emotions go once you have registered the information they are telling you. You might associate night-time and the Moon the most with peace, and believe that Water lends itself best to the feeling of peace. Once you have your item, charge intention, natural phenomena, and/or element, then you can devise *how* you will charge the item. In this instance, you could choose a cup or receptacle that has attributes you associate with peace and place within it the ring and spring water when the Moon is full.

During the full Moon, hold the cup up to the Moon, close your eyes and evoke your intention. Let your feelings of peace pour into the water. You may imagine them flowing forth as a silvery-blue light into the water and the ring glowing with peace. When you're ready, stir the water with your finger (of your dominant hand, as that is directive) in a clockwise direction. While doing so, you could say something like, 'On this calm night, I charge this ring, with the power of peace, by the full Moon's light.' Repeat as you feel necessary and when you're done, drink the peace water elixir to seal the intention, and you can wear the ring or place it upon your altar until you next wear it. Replicate this charging as often as you feel necessary.

Charge how it makes sense for you because if it doesn't resonate with you, it holds very little power. What you believe is the most important part of magick. You could charge for strength with Earth by gathering some soil, perhaps from your garden, into a metal bowl and having it sit in the full sunlight for four hours (four commonly being the number of strength). I might charge for wisdom using Air, with an incense blend of herbs and flowers I associate with clarity of thought and truth, and do so on a breezy night, during the dark Moon as that is when my intuition is more easily heard. Those are simple examples, but I hope they serve as inspiration for you.

Affirmation and New Belief Troubleshooting

If you find yourself not truly feeling an affirmation as true, notice that and work with it. You may benefit from journaling about it and potentially speaking with someone you trust and who is non-judgmental. You can ask yourself: When did I first notice myself believing the negative/unhelpful/opposite version of this affirmation? Is there someone who once told me something about this and it's kind of stuck with me ever since? Does this have anything to do with something I experienced when I was younger? Is there someone in my life I identify as being a contradiction to the new story that I want to believe?

Working through these questions should bring you closer to breaking down the old story and rewriting it so that you can tell yourself the new, more helpful version. This can be furthered with Shadow Work, which is covered in part II.

Additionally, you may find it helpful to create 'bridge statements'. They are so called because they are a step or a few steps between the negative version of the thought or belief, and the new, more positive and true version that you want to have but don't quite believe yet. So, for example, if you currently believe yourself to be ugly or gross and you want to improve your self-love, respect, worth, and value, you would want to believe the statement 'I am beautiful inside and out.' Bridges for this could be 'It's possible that not everything about me is ugly,' 'It's possible that some people do find me to be attractive,' 'It's possible that I am beautiful to some people,' 'It's possible that some things about me are beautiful,' 'Some things about me are beautiful.'

You see how these build up to the highest statement and how they stir less argument than it initially. Adopt bridge statements if you need to, because they are very helpful in actually shifting your beliefs.

Fear is not the enemy – waiting for it to end is. – Marie Forleo

Transcendental Meditation

This is a form of passive meditation that involves repeating a sound or mantra as the focus. It's a way of entering into the quiet already in your mind, and so it brings an incredible sense of connection and peace. If you resonate with mantras, you can choose one that works for you and repeat it until you feel calmer, i.e. 'I am peace and love,' or a power word, or say 'wise' on the in-breath, and 'mind' on the out-breath, or simply repeat a sound such as 'om.'

When you do this for long enough, it feels as though you can know that word or sound on a deeper level. This can be used in the morning to focus you for the day ahead or part-way through the day as a refocusing exercise when you feel the need to calm your internal world.

Create a Treasure Box and Memory Jar

Sometimes, when we're feeling low or a little out of touch with who we are, we need a reminder of where we've been and the things that have brought joy to our lives.

With a memory jar, you decorate a large jar and whenever something happens that you want to remember, write something that will jog your memory of the event or experience on a little piece of paper, roll it up and pop it into the jar.

At the year's end, review the jar and be reminded of all the lovely things that have happened and place them into an envelope marked with the year. Refill the jar each year, as this practice aids with memory consolidation and recall, and it can increase your general sense of happiness and fulfilment. There is something childlike to filling a box with wonderful things that delight us.

To make a treasure box, purchase a box that looks like a treasure chest, that is to say, a box that is beautiful to you and that you want to cherish. You can decorate a plainer box if you're a creative person, and if you're not so much, why not have a go regardless and stretch that creative muscle everyone has?

Fill your beautiful box with representations of all of the things that bring you joy and wonder. This can be photos, magazine cuttings, ticket stubs, images you draw or words that represent special things to you. Make it sensory if you can, scraps of fabric and tiny samples of scents that take you straight back to a specific time, place or person. Also place inside little trinkets that are precious, and this can also be a place to keep gratitude journals that you've filled up or the envelopes from filled annual memory jars.

Place inside literally anything you can that brings you that warm inner glow of joy. Open whenever you need a boost, feel disconnected from yourself or life, and need a reminder of who you are.

Trust yourself. You've survived a lot and you'll survive whatever is coming. – Robert Tew

SPIRIT ~ PART II

AS WITHIN, SO WITHOUT

Peace is the result of retraining your mind to process life as it is, rather than as you think it should be. – Wayne W. Dyer

***

Deepening Self-Awareness - Shadow Work

Shadow work can be thought of as almost the opposite to a gratitude practice, but it is still a part of self-care as you are essentially healing a part of you which has been hurt or is psychologically troublesome to become a more balanced version of yourself. It involves assessing why you dislike things and why particular things trigger negative emotions and toxic behaviours in you, such as anger, envy, greed, shame, guilt, pushing people away, assessing repeating patterns of behaviour and fears, uncomfortable feelings you deem inappropriate, bitterness, etc. It can also be about assessing why some positive emotions come from what most would perceive as a negative experience.

The idea is that these 'shadows' have something to teach us about ourselves and the beliefs that we operate with. They're usually telling us about our 'wilder' self that reacts from instinct, as opposed to our higher Self which responds from wisdom and love. Once we understand these, they lose some of their power, and we have more of a conscious choice as to whether we want to continue with them or not. Shadow Work is to bring the unconscious (that which is in shadow) to consciousness (that which is in light), so we can see it and respond better, or unlearn conditioning that no longer serves us.

Understanding more about the shadows of ourselves means that we can become closer to unity of the Self and so more in line with our True Self. Philosophically speaking, the True

Self is authentic, and so it operates with congruence and has more compassion because it understands how shadows form and hinder progress in life. Shadows often can be identified as various means of self-sabotage and ego-fear, so we need to bring those back towards the alignment of joy and love. This can sound very 'woo' and twee; however, these ideas are well accepted as paths to actualisation and enlightenment in transpersonal and existential psychology and philosophy. After opening my mind to it, the more I practised these things, the deeper my understanding of the concepts and the more peace I have been able to cultivate within my mind and life as a result.

Journaling is a great way to bring forth your unconscious, and aids such as tarot, certain oracle decks and archetypes can help you assess different shadows and look at them from new perspectives. The chakra or Celtic cauldron systems are also a helpful framework for looking at shadows and general wellness issues with. You can also journal using downward questioning, which is persistently taking a shadow behaviour or thought and asking 'Why?' continuously until you get to the honest root of it.

There's a reason things enter shadow as they are repressed by our conscious mind to keep ourselves safe because whatever it is was deemed too painful at the time, or there was not the mind space there to process through it. This is why things often stem from childhood – the young version of ourselves simply couldn't comprehend it or know how to handle it or soothe from it. This kind of self-development work can be painful, and you must use your own discernment for when you are ready to face these parts of yourself. It is not something to force.

It is our choices that show us what we truly are, far more than our abilities. – Albus Dumbledore

Toxic Comparison, Jealousy, and Envy

You may have heard that comparison is the thief of joy, and while that's broadly true, it's not strictly true. Comparison can be useful to help us decide on which of two or more paths will enable us to find more joy, for example. It can be useful in Shadow Work to enable us to assess what it is about someone that we admire, why and whether we really want that to be a part of ourselves, etc. This is why the word 'toxic' is often placed before comparison to differentiate it from benign comparison that isn't coming from a place of ego, fear or insecurity. Benign comparison serves as proof of possibility and leads to inspiration, which increases motivation and self-belief because then we believe that the thing we want is possible.

Toxic comparison usually takes the form of comparing oneself to another, typically in life, skill, or appearance, and leaves us feeling a mix of ashamed, left-out, hard-done-by, inferior, unworthy, sad, angry, jealous, more insecure, and bitter; and it serves to damage our self-esteem. Comparison is linked to self-esteem because those with truly high self-esteem will compare in a way that makes them feel inspired. If this isn't you, then work on your self-esteem with the practices listed throughout this book. Comparison accompanied by negative feelings means we are focusing on what we believe we don't have, which distracts from gratitude for what we do and diminishes our faith that we will and can have too.

Jealousy is recognising there is something about another person that you would also like, so it's essentially projecting your unrealised potential onto another. But envy is jealousy with the added toxicity that you believe the other person doesn't deserve what they have. This is problematic as the part of us that feels envious does so because it believes that happiness, skill, love, wealth, security, recognition, acceptance – whatever the envy is focusing on – is a finite resource. And that simply isn't true. Just because they have it doesn't mean it's not possible for us to have it too. It may not take exactly the same form as it does for them, but their having is not evidence that we can't. On the contrary, their having means it's also possible for us.

The thing is, toxic comparison, jealousy, and envy are not helpful mental activities because they simply aren't fair. We're very rarely comparing ourselves on an even footing. A flower is not concerned about the flowers next to it – it just blooms. Dig into your unconscious and feelings around this if it crops up. Apply Shadow Work principles to it, pull tarot or oracle cards around it for thought prompts and journal it out when you can give it your attention. Because these toxic feelings can often rear up when we're not in a position to suddenly whip out our journals to study what's happening, you can approach it like you would other emotions that are essentially undesirable but carrying information nonetheless: pause, acknowledge and label the emotion, and follow it up with something like, 'This indicates to me that I would like…a/more of/to feel …'. Then when you're able to, you can work on shedding light on what is behind the feeling and doing the self-development work on that.

Which do you want: the pain of staying where you are, or the pain of growth? – Judith Hanson Lasater

Current Self and Future Self Exercise

This exercise is great to do if you feel lost or unhappy in your current life and to give you clarity of how to get to your authentic life. It is helpful to make it an annual tradition to keep track of your growth and envision where you are versus where you want to be. You can do this now and mark the date for next year in a calendar or schedule to do it at a specific occasion, such as your birthday or one of the eight sabbats.

Gather some paper or your journal and colourful pens if you have them. Write the date and start with the current you – do your best to draw yourself as you look like right now; this brings realism to it. Fill around the image with how you feel right now, to create a picture of where your life is and how things are for you.

Consider: what each element represents and what's present from them right now; the state of your mind, body, and health; current challenges; work; relationships; priorities; inspirations; environment; self-care; self-love; learning; areas of growth; time-management; what you're especially grateful for.

Then move to draw the you whom you aspire to be. Write about your life a year from now and how you want to feel. Think about who is around you, your energy, community, your messages, your career. How is your life enhanced from the current you?

You could further this by writing in a journal how you can close the gaps between your current self and future self – what steps do you need to take to bring you to your ideal self in a year? What do you need to do to feel the way you want to feel more? Have a brainstorm and make a plan from there, perhaps think about planning with the Wheel of the Year, as discussed in the preparation chapter.

Dark Moon Intuition and Higher Self Ritual

This ritual can be performed annually or however often you like, to help support you with your self-development. The idea is to bring you closer to the version of yourself that you wish to be.

You will need two taper candles in secure candle holders. Use your intuition for the candle colours and whether they are both the same – if in doubt, use white. Have a toothpick, sewing needle, pin or similar object so that you can draw on the candle. Also have your signature scent oil (see page 169 for creation), personal power sigil (see page 165 for sigil creation), two pieces of paper, a pen, and a cauldron or fire-safe bowl. You may also like to burn an incense or oil that corresponds to the trait you wish to focus on.

Prepare the scene and ensure that you can see well by candlelight and cast a circle. Position the two pillar candles as far apart as you safely can on the altar surface. Take one of the two pieces of paper and write the traits and abilities that you currently feel that you have and place it under one of the candles. Take this candle and draw on it your power sigil.

On the other piece of paper, duplicate what you have already written and write another trait or quality that you are currently working on developing. Write in the positive, so for example, if you are working on being less stubborn write instead 'flexible mind', or if you're focusing on not saying yes to things that don't serve you, you may write 'assertive'.

Place this paper under the other candle and take that candle and draw on it your personal power sigil and write the word you've chosen on the candle as well, starting at the wick. Take your signature scent oil and anoint the candle with a few drops of it, starting at the wick again.

Ensure both candles are secured in their holders and light the first candle (the one without the word written on).

Enter a meditative state, which you can do either with your eyes closed or by gazing softly at the lit candle. As you breathe in the scent of the power oil, see the version of you that possesses the trait or quality that you have chosen. Feel into this and see yourself acting as if this quality is present.

When you feel ready, open your eyes and say 'I am [trait/quality], and so it is,' or 'I am of [trait/quality], and so it is' (whichever is appropriate for your phrasing). Snuff the lit flame and close the circle when you're ready.

The next night, cast your circle again if you feel called to and when you are calm and ready, light the same candle again, this time moving it a little closer to the other candle while saying 'I am … and so it is.' Repeat this every night until the Moon is full or until your candle reaches the candle with the word inscribed.

Once you reach the other candle, use the flame of the lit candle to light the other candle and as you do so, see the quality/trait you desired being a part of you. See the spark of the quality that you started with and how you have seen that spark grow as you have nurtured it and that it now resides within you, as a part of who you are. Feel the gratitude you have for this trait. Sit with this feeling.

Carefully burn the first piece of paper and let it burn out in a cauldron. Extinguish the flames and whenever you wish to feel into that trait again, light the candle with its inscription for as long as it lasts. Alternatively, you can let both candles safely burn out.

Any time you wish to use this ritual in future, use the paper that remains as the starting point and place that under the candle that doesn't have the trait desired written on. This way, you don't need to start from scratch every time. Store the paper somewhere safe, perhaps in a manifestation box or your Book of Shadows.

Your whole life is a creative activity. – Elizabeth Gilbert

Self-Dedication Ritual

This is a simple personal ritual where you dedicate yourself to bringing your current self into alignment with your Highest Self. Dedication rituals are often performed when there's a need to rededicate oneself to their path. It is an act of affirming that you acknowledge the changes ahead and that they are bringing you closer to your True Self. It is often performed skyclad (nude/one with the sky) and in a safe, tranquil place or before your altar.

Perform on the Moon phase that feels right to you and/or the day of the week that you feel best lends itself to this type of ritual – for me, it's a waxing Moon for growth and Monday for divine femininity and all things Moon-related.

In terms of ingredients for this ritual, you will choose (or pre-make) those that best represent your Highest Self: an essential oil or oil blend (safe to touch the skin, perhaps the signature scent from page 169), incense, a votive candle, water, blessed salt (as described on page 27), and a drink of your choice.

It can also be lovely to create a playlist of music that you feel really connects you to yourself and your purpose and play this during the ritual to deepen your experience.

Cast a circle and take a moment to mentally prepare for the ritual, listening to your chosen music.

Light the incense and disrobe when you're ready.

Sprinkle the salt onto the floor so that you may stand upon it, and light the ritual candle.

You will firstly anoint yourself with the water, then the drink of your choosing, and oil, each in turn. So, you will repeat the anointing and invocation three times in total.

Take the water to anoint firstly, and say the following:

'Bless me Universe/Cosmos/God, for I am your child.'

'Blessed be my eyes, that I may see my path.'

Anoint your third eye.

'Blessed be my nose, that I may breathe freely.'

Anoint your nose.

'Blessed be my mouth, that I may speak my truth.'

Anoint your lips (be careful when it's the oil to not consume any).

'Blessed be my ears, that I may hear my intuition and guides.'

Anoint your ear lobes.

'Blessed be my heart, that I may be faithful in my work and act always from a place of love and peace.'

Anoint your heart area.

'Blessed be my loins, which bring forth life from my ancestors.'

Carefully anoint your upper mons pubis.

'Blessed be my feet, that I may walk in love and joy.'

Anoint your feet.

Repeat with the drink, and lastly with your oil.

You may then finish your drink whilst you hold your intention and reflect on your experience within this ritual, and close when you're ready.

Be sure to journal your experiences afterwards, perhaps in your Book of Mirrors if you have one.

Card Spread: Make a Difference, by Kelly-Ann Maddox

This spread is great for when you want to make a difference with your choices and life and be of service, but are feeling a little overwhelmed by choice or just can't decide which direction may be the right one to go in. It can also be used to tap in occasionally to reassess what you're doing with this area.

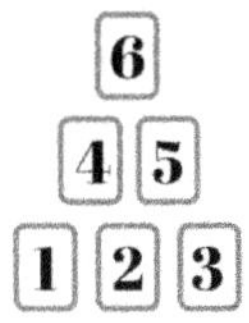

1. Possible causes or issues that could be calling to my heart currently.
2. Effective steps to take in the coming weeks.
3. Strengths and abilities which help me to make a difference.
4. Possible issues I may face and how to tackle them.
5. Types of action and advocacy which could suit me and my lifestyle.
6. A symbol of power to encourage me in taking the first steps.

All change is hard at first, messy in the middle, and gorgeous in the end. – Robin Sharma

The following journal prompts lead on from this spread because having a sense of direction is a crucial part of wellness that is often missed. It's been said that a human without a purpose is like a ship lost at sea – blown here and there by the wind and tossed fruitlessly by the waves. It can't be minimised that the majority of humans find some peace in having a sense of purpose, and there is no one way of discovering purpose. The journey to fulfilment of one's purpose is often the point of the purpose itself. Be aware that your purpose can change or become more refined, but that only occurs once you start walking and living it. We all care about different areas of our life, and we are most likely to have different purposes in each area. You're a multi-faceted being – you don't have to be limited to just one!

Particularly in my darker times, I've gotten stuck in meaning and meaninglessness, and it was really hard to break free from that and try to see a different perspective. I know I was one of the 'lucky ones' in the sense that I *was* able to give enough momentary spotlight to that part of me that believed there was actually *something,* even if I didn't know what it was or what I was 'looking for' and take that leap of faith into the unknown.

In time I was able to work on my need to know everything and basically control through fear – fear of the unknown. An important part of mental health is tolerance of ambiguity. I was able to accept that I would not know everything and could not control everything. Getting really honest with myself, I didn't actually want to know or control everything. Part of the beauty of life was in the random, the things I could not predict or imagine, and experiencing that *is* living. I got comfortable with being uncomfortable, and two huge parts of that ability were developing my trust in myself and the Universe.

Spending time to get to know the younger generation helped me as well. I think connecting with people that weren't already a part of my life was actually what was helpful, even though I didn't realise it at the time. I met some amazing young people through my volunteering who inspired me and made me want to somehow advocate for better, and I still meet them now in my work. These amazing people deserved to grow up in the best world that they can, and as an adult, I could *help* to bring that world closer.

So, until you can get to the point of accepting you may not know anything for certain, the idea is to find the anchors – the things you *can* believe in that give you *a* purpose, even if it's not *the* purpose, and work on your sense of trust. Some of the following questions should help you.

It's also helpful to note that even if you discover a personality trait that you are not keen on about yourself or you do not love for some reason, perhaps because it seems to cause problems for you, that is doesn't matter – as personality is not fixed. Humans are very flexible, can learn new ways of being whenever they choose to, and a lot of this is due to neuroplasticity. I used to be stubborn, and now I am flexible, but I can use my inherent stubbornness to my advantage whenever I choose to. I also used to be shy, but I learnt to be confident, and now I embrace my natural tendency to be reserved. Take the trait and look at what its opposite is, then figure out a way to walk the middle path between the two extremes. When you're able to do that, you will be able to use either side to your advantage whenever a situation calls for it. This is self-mastery in action.

Other traits may be talked about often in a negative light, such as sensitivity. There's always a balance within a trait so that it is expressed in a way that serves your highest good. Sensitivity is a gift that allows you to feel compassion and experience life deeply – that can be seen as a gift or a curse – it's up to you to decide which it is.

Spirit Journal/Meditation and Refection Prompts:

~What does spirituality really mean to me?

~What is magick to me – how would I define it?

~What are my current strengths in my spirituality/magick?

~How can I develop my spirituality and/magick further?

~What does my ideal morning look like?

~What does my ideal bedtime look like?

~What would a 'perfect' day be for me?

~What does my ideal week look like?

~What do I need to implement daily for my self-care?

~What do I need to do weekly for my self-care?

~What special things can I plan throughout my year to give me continual things to look forward to?

~Where do I want to be within my life in a year's time?

~What type of future do I want for myself?

~What does this future need so it can come into my life?

~What type of world do I want to live in – and how am I already making this desired reality a lived tangible reality?

~What do I want to do before I leave this Earth?

~Is there something I have always dreamed of doing that I haven't done yet – what is it and can I start or do it now?

~What gives me real satisfaction?

~What types of advocacy suit me and my lifestyle?

~What do I feel that I am, at this time, here to learn?

~What am I currently here to teach?

~How can I spread my message kindly and effectively?

~What abilities and strengths do I possess that will help me with my purpose or mission?

~How should my inner world be if I am in alignment with my highest purpose?

~What steps do I need to take to come into alignment with my highest purpose? (Working backwards helps!)

~What would bring me elevation?

~What are my current problem areas/weak points?

~What do I need to avoid moving forwards, and why?

~What positive changes can I consider making at present?

~How can I fully embrace who I am now?

~How can I be more dedicated and consistent?

~What commitments do I need to make to myself?

~What is one key short-term action, implementable immediately, to help me strengthen my connection to my inner passion?

~What fresh ideas do I have that I can follow soon?

~What do I need to know to be happier?

~What skills do I need to live a better life?

Maybe I am an investment. Not in the way of new cars and houses, Maybe I am an antique thing, that struggles but somehow still manages to keep ticking. Abandoned, worn, yes. But with care, with time: grand, intricate, full of stories. Full of life. – McKenna Kaelin

9 ~ PARTING THOUGHTS

I am not looking to escape my darkness, I am learning to love myself there. – Rune Lazuli

I hope that after reading each of the previous chapters of this book, you see how magickal you are as a person, and how magick can support you in your wellness and your journey of becoming your True Self. Working with the natural cycles of the solar system and Earth is part of the life of a witch, and it is through this understanding that we deepen our awareness of our own cycles and rhythms. The more we understand the world around us, the better we know how to operate within it. The lessons we observe we can apply to ourselves, gaining more wisdom at each turn. As we appreciate how the natural cycles support us, we become much more inclined to care for them back.

There are many, many lessons contained within each of the elements, and while you have likely learnt many already in your life, the work of learning is never done. We face new situations and new circumstances every day. These are all but opportunities for learning and growth.

Earth teaches us to foremost respect our body for it houses our spirit. This will be shown in how we speak about, speak to, and treat our body, ensuring that we nurture it and give it what it needs to be healthy and strong. It asks us to be mindful of our physical environment and curate it so that it best supports us. Earth also teaches us patience for most plants to not bear fruit overnight, and we may need to put a lot of effort and trust into an endeavour before it yields what we desire. Earth challenges us to be strong and steadfast with our dreams yet hold them with care so that they are not crushed before they have a chance to blossom. It also reminds us that we can grow through challenges and become even more self-mastered.

Water asks us to connect with our emotions and heed what it is they are telling us. There is a subtle balance between witnessing the emotion and learning from it so that we can choose our next steps wisely. We do not ignore feelings and bury them somewhere hidden that they might trip us up later; nor do we want to overly engage with them and bring them too close so that we cannot see anything else and risk becoming overrun with them and lose sight of reason. As Osho wisely connected, *emotion* reflects that they are in constant motion or flow and so we must learn to move with them – very much like being balanced on a surfboard.

Water invites us to nourish our connections with others and find a balance of emotional honesty within them that we are comfortable with so that we can relate to one another on a human-to-human level. We are encouraged to learn to ride the waves of emotions as they come and go, whether they be high or low, long-lasting or short-lived. Deep and fathomless Water welcomes us to engage with our intuition – our internal deep sense of knowing – and learn to trust ourselves implicitly. As our connection to our Higher Self grows, so does our ability to discern our intuition from any ego that may be misguided.

The world needs that special gift that only you have.
– Marie Forleo

Air teaches us that our thoughts are powerful and create our reality, past, present, and future. We learn that our mind is both a canvas and a manuscript, and we weave our story onto them. Because we hold the brush and the pen, we can re-create our story and ourselves at any point we wish. If we have outgrown a version of ourselves, we can change the wardrobe whenever we want to; we just have to make the decision and take the steps.

Just as incense smoke and hot breath on a cold day dissipates almost instantly into the air around it, Air reminds us to be careful with our language and to take time often to be mindful. Because when we are mindful, we can listen to our body and heart and know what is going on for ourselves physically and emotionally. This awareness allows us to make wiser decisions moving forwards and be more likely to act from the highest version of ourselves.

Fire is the spark of creation and action. It's taught us about our personal joy and values and the things that are most important to us. It builds on the other elements because without them there, Fire's passion cannot burn well or safely. If we are worrying about our foundation and stability or have lost our roots, then Fire may not be able to ignite – where is our happiness if we do not have our basic needs met or a rudimentary sense of stability? If our emotions are running amok, then we risk Fire getting drowned in a cacophony of emotions and losing our direction. If we are not clear with our intent for Fire, we could get blown in the wrong direction or become hyper-focused into a passion at the expense of everything else and risk burning out, or risk it all burning down in a colossal blaze.

Fire is a most wonderous element, but it needs the most temperance, for its powers of destruction can be the quickest to ignite and the hardest to quell. Fire teaches us to balance and tend to a flame, fully being present with only as much as we can handle at any one time. We are encouraged to allow Fire to warm us and so fill ourselves with courage and the sense of power that we need to make our dreams realised.

Your shadow is not the part of you that is 'bad'; it's the part of you that needs more love. – Erin Telford

Spirit is everything at its core. It is the unification of all and at the same time, the highest expression of each as its unique self. Spirit teaches us to be mindful of the bigger picture, both of our lives and of others. Our life is ours to live, yet we are not technically separate to others. We are part of a collective. We are products of our place in time, but that does not mean that we are any less powerful or capable of change – in fact, it makes us more so because we are more aware and can choose to be our authentic Self at any point.

Spirit asks us to consider going beyond ourselves where and when we can. To step up and be of service in the ways that make the best use of our own unique gifts, abilities, skills and talents. Spirit asks us to find and create balance within our lives, emotions, mind, and heart, and reminds us that we will each have a blend that is unique to us.

Your personal landscape is yours to shape as you will. If you don't like a plant where it is, gently move it to a new home – you can always change your perspective with something until it fits somewhere that works for you. If a weed pops up that strangles the flowers you diligently nurtured from seed, throw that weed onto the compost so that it might make way for something better - you have the power to send unwanted thoughts and images on their way.

Hopefully, through the journal prompts and exercises throughout this book, you have deepened your self-awareness and improved your self-esteem as you realise that you have gotten yourself through a lot so far in your life, so, you *can* trust yourself. You are eternally casting yourself – you *are* the spell. Your life is your making. *You* are your making.

Ultimately, it matters not what happened yesterday or happens tomorrow; what matters most always is what happens in the present – now. Magick is in the moment. Magick is now. It is here and now. Use it to the best of your abilities at this moment, learn the lessons as they come up, and strive to do better next time.

Your best self is magnificent, and today, you are already the best version of you that you have ever been. No version of you knows what you know today. Keep riding that forward momentum and take the pressure off yourself to be the best right now or know all of the things right now. Pressure is downwards and is ultimately slowing, but little steps are forward momentum; one thing at a time keeps the flow. Continue following your joy with a light heart, and you won't go far wrong.

Everything mentioned in this book can take practice, but everything mentioned has real promise of benefit for you, and I trust that you have already felt great benefits from whatever things you have tried so far. Maybe not everything has been relevant to you at this time, but at the very least I hope that you have learnt some tools that you can pass onto others who may need to hear them or could benefit from them.

Understand your darkness and you'll be consumed by your light.
– Cassie Uhl

I would like to leave you with one last quote, which is one of my ultimate favourite quotes from the astounding Elizabeth Gilbert in her book *Big Magic*, 'The Universe buries strange jewels deep within us all and then stands back to see if we can ever find them. The hunt to uncover those jewels, that's creative living. The courage to go on that hunt in the first place – that's what separates a more mundane existence from an enchanted one. The often surprising results of that hunt – that's what I call big magic.' We all have the seeds of potential within us, and it is up to us if we take the time to nurture those seeds so that they might become the captivating flowers and the great trees that we dream of. We need only hope and then decide to act upon that hope, riding the waves of life as they ebb and flow.

I still cannot quite believe that this book is real; as I type these final few words, I thank you again, dear reader, for you choosing this book and I hope that it has given you what you were looking for – inspiration, help with your self-development – whatever it was, I hope that the words, exercises, and rituals within these pages serve you for many years to come. Wherever your path may lead you next, perhaps you'll take a look at some of the resources listed at the back of this book, or somewhere else entirely … No matter where you go, I wish you well, and I hope that you are forevermore your true magickal self.

10 ~ RESOURCES

1. Ambika Winters: *The Complete Guide to Chakras*
2. Carl Rogers: *On Becoming A Person* (person-centred life)
3. Carolyn Myss: *Archetype Cards* (Jungian psychospirituality)
4. Claire Johnson: *Llewellyn's Complete Book of Lucid Dreaming*
5. Christopher Penczak: *The Inner Temple of Witchcraft*
6. Christopher Titmus: *Meditation Healing* (mindfulness)
7. Colin Espie: *Overcoming Insomnia and Sleep problems*
8. Daniel Kahneman: *Thinking, Fast and Slow* (cognition)
9. Derren Brown: *Happy* (philosophy, science and wisdom)
10. Edain McCoy: *Advanced Witchcraft* (a grounded perspective)
11. Elaine N. Aron: *The Highly Sensitive Person* (empaths)
12. Elizabeth Gilbert: *Big Magic* (creativity and inspiration)
13. Emma Mumford: *Spiritual Queen* (spirituality and self-love)
14. Erica Feldmann: *Haus Magick* ("Cottage" Witchcraft)
15. Fiona Horne: *The Art of Witch* (for 'higher minded' witches)
16. Gabrielle Bernstein: *The Universe Has Your Back* (spiritual)
17. Gelong Thubten: *A Monk's Guide to Happiness* (meditation)

18. Hal Elrod: *The Miracle Morning* (effective morning routines)
19. James Clear: *Atomic Habits* (creating habits and systems)
20. Jude C. Todd: *Herbal Home Remedies* (herbs for medicine)
21. Kelly-Ann Maddox: *Youtube and online as: The Four Queens*
22. Lucy H. Pearce: *Moon Time* (spirituality and menstruation)
23. Marie Kondo: *Spark Joy* (decluttering and organising)
24. Minerva Siegel: *Tarot for Self-Care* (tarot explanations)
25. Phyllis Curott: *Book of Shadows* (autobiography of a witch)
26. Rebecca Campbell: *Light is the New Black* (spirituality)
27. Silija: *The Green Wiccan Herbal* (herbs and their uses)
28. Simon Sinek: *Start with Why* (motivation and habit creation)
29. Soraya: *The Kitchen Witch* (herbs practical and magickal)
30. Stephen D. Famer: *Earth Magic* (Shamanism and magick)
31. Steve Hagen: *Buddhism Plain and Simple* (meditation)
32. Susan Jeffers: *Feel the Fear and do it Anyway* (anxiety help)
33. Todd Herman: *The Alter Ego Effect* (archetype working)
34. Maisie Hill: *Period Power* (menstruation and hormones)
35. Michelle L. Glendenhuys: *A Guide to Shadow Work*

ABOUT THE AUTHOR

Sophie's mission is about blending spirituality with evidence-based psychological treatments and understanding to create an integrative balance of wellness, unique to each individual. She believes in life-long learning and personal development within all aspects of a person's life in order to live authentically, with more balance and love. Sophie works as a registered psychotherapist and counsellor, offering services in-person and worldwide online. She also works as a life coach and Usui reiki practitioner and has been intentionally spiritual and practising magick since 2002.

Sophie started her work in the mental health field in 2012 by volunteering at a domestic abuse shelter, which led her on a path to complete a master's in forensic psychology and eventually train further as a counsellor. Private practice has allowed her the freedom to work holistically with each client and look at their whole world, tailoring each session to best meet their individual needs.

For complementary resources to this book, you can find Sophie online at www.sophiewildrobin.com.

 @sophiewildrobin

 @sophierobinsonmatthews

Positivi-tea and Talk

Photo credit above: Rachael Day @rachday_
Photo credit backcover: Ellie Mae Moreing @ellie_mae_designs

CPSIA information can be obtained
at www.ICGtesting.com
Printed in the USA
BVHW041659100820
586039BV00016B/192